an apple for the teacher

A Teachers' Lounge Paranormal Romance

Teachers' Lounge
Book One

deelylah mullin

Cover art: Maddie James

Editing: Catharine Bijak

Purple Pen Wordsmithing, LLC, acknowledges the following registered trademarks used in the text of this novel:

- Kool-Aid ® Kraft Foods, Inc.
- Spaghetti-Os ® CSC Brands LP
- Styrofoam ® The Dow Chemical Company

For everyone who's dreamed about living in a community where they are accepted for who they are unconditionally.

I created Zephyr for us.

heads up

Zephyr, Michigan has been designed to be a utopia—where everyone is accepted for who they are, despite what is going on in the Real World.

Regardless of living in this idealistic world, characters still have baggage.

In *An Apple for the Teacher*, please note the following content warnings:

- Emotional abuse from a partner (discussed, not explicit)
- Gaslighting
- Physical abuse from a partner (discussed, not explicit)

Welcome to Zephyr, Michigan—a seemingly ordinary town with an extraordinary secret. Behind the façade of small-town life, supernatural Beings walk among unsuspecting humans. Witches, vampires, shifters, and fae call Zephyr home, carefully governed by a town council dedicated to maintaining harmony between all residents.

But it's in the most unexpected place that love finds a way to bridge two worlds. At Zephyr Junior/Senior High, the teachers' lounge becomes the unlikely backdrop for blooming romances. As hearts race and sparks fly, dangerous secrets threaten to unravel the delicate balance of this unique community.

Dive into this captivating paranormal romance series where love, suspense, and supernatural intrigue collide. Will these budding relationships survive the challenges of a world where magic lurks just beneath the surface? Discover the enchanting tales of Zephyr, where every stolen glance in the teachers' lounge could be the beginning of a mystical love story.

chapter one

Dinah glanced at the clock before continuing, "Esteemed humans, that's it for today. Please remember to complete the next section in chapter three as homework and review your notes from the first two sections. I expect some topics for presentations tomorrow!"

Layla, one of her best students, approached her. "Ms. James? I have a family obligation and I don't think I'll have my topic ready on time."

Grinning, Dinah said, "Oh, Layla. Don't worry about it. Are you going to see your grandparents tonight?"

The teen nodded, her excitement evident. "I am. We've got this huge thing and they're both super excited to see all of us."

"Well, tell them I said 'hi.' And your parents, too. Get that concept to me by the end of the week."

"Absolutely. I really appreciate it." Layla's grin was a brilliant white and almost blinded Dinah before she spun and jogged out the doorway, joining her friends in the hall.

Which dentist does she go to? I need sunglasses when she's smiling.

She glanced at her desk. Her favorite coffee mug, professing her love of the Oxford comma, sat empty, waiting for her to haul it down the hallway and refill it. She grabbed the cold ceramic and cradled it in the crook of her opposite arm.

And it was only mid-September. *This'll be a long school year.*

As she rounded the corner, a group of football players huddled near one of the eleventh grader's lockers. Raucous laughter burst from the boys.

"Dude, I *dare* you to tell Coach how you spent the weekend!"

More laughter.

A different voice. "You're going to be doing line drills until you puke!"

Across the hall, a boy with a forlorn expression looked at the gathering. Dinah almost felt him reaching out to be included as one of the *brothers*.

The neon *Coming Soon* sign caught her attention as she continued down the hallway.

See this modern retelling of one of the Bard's most
humorous tales.
Stage play by Anthony Newman and Faith James
Directed by Kennedy Armbruster; Layla Timmons; and
faculty advisor, Arlan DeSalvo

Three performances. *Another weekend in the theater. It could be worse—she might have chosen an outdoor activity.*

"Dinah! I just *love* that necklace! It brings out the green hints in your eyes," Mara Slade, the art teacher, chirped, as she rounded the corner where hallways intersected. "Wherever did you find it? We should shop together sometime because we have the same tastes." She slid her arm around Dinah's as they walked hip-to-hip along the familiar path to the teachers' lounge.

For crappy coffee.

"We *should* go shopping. Sometime when Faith is out of town, we will." Dinah tried to muster at least a little enthusiasm for the woman who had become her closest friend in Zephyr.

But they weren't *that* close.

Dinah didn't let others in. She couldn't. Not if she wanted to keep her peaceful life the way it was. *It has to be this way.*

"...so, I definitely think we should go into Petoskey this weekend and take in the last outdoor concert of the year. The band is supposed to be good," Mara said.

"Faith—"

"Bring her with us. It's not like she's a bratty kid or anything. She's pretty cool, if you ask me." Mara opened the door to the lounge.

Making a beeline for the restaurant-grade coffee maker, Dinah groaned.

"Ut oh. Someone didn't make coffee. I sense an email brewing in that brilliant brain of yours." Mara chuckled and used the tap on the side to fill her cup with hot water. She likely had some new herbal tea, which was her absolute favorite *ever*.

"You know, it's not that big a deal. I don't mind—and there was enough for me." Dinah grinned. "But woe to the person who arrives for a refill before the pot is done," she said as she dumped out the spent grounds and reset the brewer.

The door opened and there he was. Arlan DeSalvo. The recently hired advanced math teacher. The guy was sex-on-a-stick as far as Dinah was concerned. A long tunnel reached between the two of them, and she connected with the younger man. Until a single word interrupted her train of thought.

Mara whispered, "Breathe." Then, she addressed the newcomer, "Hey, Arlan. How's it going with all the high-level math classes?"

He chuckled. "Well, we're still reviewing, but I think they all have a great understanding of the content they should know." He turned his brilliant smile on Dinah. "You've converted me. I'm now a fan of the Oxford comma." He pointed at her mug.

She grinned as heat crept up her neck. "Yup. But I took the last of the coffee. Sorry. Whomever finished the other pot didn't bother to make more." She took in the white chip in the sage ceramic cup latched around his index finger. His hands were beautiful. She imagined him floating his long fingers over a piano keyboard playing Chopin in the living room as she painted in the sunporch of her home.

"That's okay. I have some bottled water in the mini-fridge in my room. I'll survive until after the next class." He glanced at the floor and back up at her. "You look lovely in that shade of pink. I think the green stones in your necklace make your eyes sparkle." He pressed his lips together before he turned on his heel and exited the lounge.

Dinah exhaled. Aloud.

"Did you *hear* that? Ohmygod. He *likes* you!" Mara continued to ramble on in the softest whisper she could manage. Which wasn't very quiet.

"Mara? You know I love you, right?"

"I do. What's up?" she asked as a crease formed between her eyebrows.

"I wish you wouldn't make such a big deal out of what Mr. DeSalvo said. It's not like I could *do* anything about it, anyway." Dinah opened the door and slipped into the hallway with Mara close at her heels.

"Why not?" Mara asked once she'd caught up, and they walked shoulder-to-shoulder. "Oh, how could I forget? You're a martyr and you think you can't have a life because you have Faith. Well, let me tell you, you aren't doing her any favors by doting on her. Being at her disposal."

"It's not like that. I'm just...protective." Dinah and Faith were almost always together when school was out—when Faith wasn't on a trip for drama Dinah couldn't chaperone. Which didn't happen often.

"I get that. But you're not happy, are you?" Mara stopped her in the hallway and faced her. "Really, Dinah. Every time Faith is gone, you mope. It's like you've built your life around her and now that she has a life of her own —without you—it seems like you're lost. Start doing stuff with other people. Put yourself out there. It doesn't have to be romantic, but what if it turns out to be?" Mara searched Dinah's eyes. "You deserve to be happy, too."

"I'll think about it. In the meantime, don't meddle." Dinah looked at Mara and pointed. "I mean it."

The glint in Mara's eyes dimmed a smidge. "You sure

know how to spoil a girl's fun. I'm off!" She waved her arm in a grandiose sweep and floated down the hallway with her multicolored skirt rippling and the long sweater she wore flapping at her sides as her Birkenstocks slapped against her heels.

Dinah made it into her classroom a moment before the bell rang as her students quieted and settled in their seats. "I've got coffee. Let's get busy talking about ancient Greece."

YOU LOOK *lovely in that shade of pink. I think the green stones in your necklace make your eyes sparkle.* "How lame," Arlan muttered under his breath as he stared at the dark grout surrounding the darker ceramic tile as he moved down the hallway toward his classroom.

"Hey, Mr. DeSalvo!"

Arlan picked his head up, scanning his surroundings.

A bulky guy with hair like a raven's wing crossed the hallway in three long steps. Thomas Stebbins, the king of the football team's defense, smiled ear-to-ear as he adjusted his stride to match Arlan's. "I know we're early in the school year, but I am majorly struggling with calc. Do you think you could recommend a tutor or find time for me when I don't have practice?"

Arlan glanced at the senior's profile. Classic good looks, great hair, and charm for days. "I suppose I could make sure I carve out some time in the mornings—before school starts—to work with you."

The man-boy clapped him on the back. "Mr. DeSalvo,

sir, thank you so much. Can I come in tomorrow morning, and we can figure out where I screwed up my homework?"

Standing outside his classroom door, Arlan said, "I can make that happen. I'm usually here by seven. See you then?"

Thomas' jaw dropped. "S-seven? In the morning? Gee, Mr. DeSalvo, class doesn't start until eight. I get up at quarter after seven...."

The panic that swept across the boy's face made a gleeful chortle bubble up from Arlan's diaphragm, but he contained it. "Gotcha! I was kidding. I'm not even back from my run until you get up. See me at lunch or right after school and we'll work out a time. I'm sure your coach would understand if you were late to practice a couple times a week, so you remained eligible to play."

The color drained from Thomas' face.

"Ha ha ha. Just messin' with you. We'll figure out a time. Now, go to class, so you're not late."

With a nod, Thomas jogged off and rounded the corner, heading into the science wing.

Maybe he can give me pointers so I can talk to Dinah instead of putting my foot in my mouth. Arlan had seen girls draping themselves all over Thomas, but the boy didn't have a girlfriend as far as he could tell. But he was friends with everyone. On second thought, Thomas might not be the best choice for a teenaged mentor.

Sighing, he walked into his classroom and slid the chipped mug onto his desk. *Maybe Dinah will be in the lounge looking for more coffee after this hour.* He daydreamed for a minute as he logged into his computer and pulled up the slideshow previewing the order of operations and axioms of arithmetic for his algebra two class.

Dinah drifted across the wooded landscape wrapped in a forest green cloak. Her eyes glimmered in the haze of the setting sun slipping into the large lake....

The bell announcing the beginning of the period startled him from the vision—the same one from the recurring dream he'd been having ever since he'd met the curvaceous history teacher.

He'd been touring the school with the principal, Janae Brown, when Dinah had jogged from her classroom shouting, "Mara, get down here and finish what you started!" The pinked apples of her cheeks highlighted her smile—which lit up the dark hallway in the English wing.

Ms. Brown had cleared her throat and Dinah had stopped in her tracks. "Oh. I'm sorry. I didn't realize there were others in the building today. Mara and I are working on bulletin boards—rather, Mara is starting them with an epic vision and leaving me to muck them up." She smiled—a shy upturning of her lips—then reached out her right hand to Arlan. "I'm Dinah James, and I promise I don't run in the hallways when there are students here."

Arlan took the proffered appendage and wrapped his fingers around her soft skin. It had been like time had frozen and his gaze fixed on Dinah, taking in her features, and committing them to memory.

Clearing her throat again, Ms. Brown had said, "Ms. James teaches history and has a daughter in eleventh grade attending Zephyr High." Addressing the flustered history educator, the principal said,

"Mr. DeSalvo will fill our advanced math vacancy. He's also certified to teach theater arts and biology, so I'm sure you'll eventually cross paths."

"I— Um, you'll love it here, Mr. DeSalvo—"

"Arlan. Call me Arlan when class isn't in session."

She beamed. "I'd like that. Let me know if you have any questions or need to find anything around here. I know the low-down." Dinah relaxed and extracted her hand from his. "Enjoy the rest of your tour." She stepped away from them and addressed Ms. Brown. "If you see Mara, please communicate that it'd be great if she came down here. I could use her help."

"Certainly. Don't work too long today—we've got all next week to get things done," the administrator said.

"Oh, I'm going to make some coffee—I've got a few hours before Faith returns from a camping trip with the Timmons."

"It was nice meeting you, Dinah. Enjoy your day, and thanks for the offer—I'm sure I'll have tons of questions as soon as I get my bearings."

He'd walked away with Ms. Brown, continuing the tour of the facility. They'd ended up in his classroom—a math lab outfitted with state-of-the-art technology and manipulatives. But even the shiny smart board couldn't keep him focused on complex math concepts and his new position.

"I think you have everything you need, Arlan. Keys to your classroom and the storage room, computer access, and your assigned laptop are on the desk over there." Ms. Brown inclined her head away from him. "Feel free to settle in and let us know if we can help you with anything. I'll see you officially next week. Welcome to Zephyr." She spun on her heel and strode, with purpose, out the door.

The excitement of finding a teaching position had been no match for Dinah James' capri-length jeans, which hugged her ample curves, topped with a Bon Jovi T-shirt which showcased her magnificent breasts.

"Mr. DeSalvo? Can I use the bathroom?" Faith James asked.

He blinked several times before she came into view. "Oh, uh, certainly. Take a pass." He gestured toward the large pink Pi symbol hanging from a hook near the door.

"Thank you, sir." She crossed the room with rapid steps, taking the pass with her.

"Okay, folks. Let's get started. Today, we're going to talk about axioms."

After he'd made it through several slides and given the students a task, he moved to the front of the room and took a bottle of water from the mini-fridge on the floor behind his desk. He brought the container to his lips and relished the refreshing liquid in his parched mouth.

His mouth was always parched around Dinah. It was like she drew every ounce of moisture from him—or evaporated it away—whenever he saw or thought about her.

"Sorry to interrupt, Mr. DeSalvo," Dinah said as she walked into the room carrying a full carafe of coffee. "Just wanted to make sure you got some of this." She smiled and reached for his mug.

Arlan beat her to it. "Thank you. Here," —he reached for the pot— "let me."

Their fingers brushed as he slid his around the handle and that same pull surged through his arm—the one he'd yearned for since the first time he'd met her. Hiding a boner in front of a class of high school students—especially when he needed to move about to assist them with the paragraph he'd asked them to write about mathematical rules—proved difficult.

She smiled.

He filled his cup and set the pot on his desk a little too hard. The dark liquid sloshed in the carafe. Focused on the hot bean water, Arlen willed it not to spill over the top. The remaining coffee stilled almost immediately. *Weird.* He shook off the strange behavior of the fluid. "You didn't have to do this—it's so kind of you. Thank you."

Dinah shrugged. "Not a big deal. I snuck out for more and thought I'd share for a change." Taking the container, she said, "Gotta get back. See you at lunch?"

Arlan nodded. "Definitely. I'll need more coffee by then."

She laughed as she palmed the handle of the carafe. "Hoping all the students have real and not imaginary homework."

He shook his head. "That's so bad." Dinah sighed and the roll of her hips as she sashayed out the door and down the hall entranced him.

"Mr. DeSalvo? Do you have a thing for Faith's *mom*?"

He didn't know who said it, but Arlan froze. Ice crept up his chest and snaked up his neck and over his scalp.

When he turned and looked around the room, Faith had put her head face down on her desk with her hoodie pulled up and most of the classroom had a shocked expression.

"Ms. James is a colleague. Nothing more." *At this time. I hope that'll change—and soon.*

chapter two

"We are *not* having this discussion, Faith. It's one hundred percent none of your business."

"The hell it isn't. Mom, you have *no* idea what it's like with a parent working at the school you go to." Faith shoved her spaghetti squash with marinara toward the center of the table. "And you didn't have to sit in class watching adults flirt over coffee."

Leaning a generous hip against the counter, Dinah sighed. "Nothing is going on, and I'm not flirting with him. Just...leave it alone, okay?"

"Mara says you have a thing for him. In what reality is a twenty-something-year-old guy going to date an over-forty woman?" Faith stood and took the remains of her dinner into the kitchen, scraped them into the compost bin, and rinsed her plate.

She turned toward Dinah. "He's hot, mom. Think about it. You're probably not his type, anyway. He runs five miles each morning. Most of the juniors and seniors attracted to his type know the route he takes." The teen rolled her eyes and launched herself at her mother, wrapping her arms around her waist. "There are people taking pictures of him without his shirt on and sharing them far and wide." She sighed. "I don't want to see you get hurt, Mumma. Boys are stupid—you keep telling me that. And Mr. DeSalvo isn't much older than the seniors." Faith gave her a tight squeeze before loosening her grip and dropping her arms, playing nonchalant—as if she hadn't just let it slip that she cared about her mom.

"I know, kiddo." Dinah turned away, trying to couch her expression and hide her disappointment. "I'm more realistic than you and Mara give me credit for. It's still nice to flirt with him, though."

She paused, then added, "And Mr. DeSalvo is almost thirty—twenty-nine, to be exact. His birthday is in February."

Faith rolled her eyes. "As long as flirting is all it is. I mean, if you're interested and he's interested, please do me a favor and wait until after I graduate?"

Dinah sighed.

"I mean, I guess you should wait. I don't know—it's not fair for me to ask that of you if you're both interested." Faith paced behind her, twirling a lock of hair around her index finger—a sure sign she was having a tough time making a decision.

Dinah turned. "My only concern, since your birth, has been you. And my focus will stay on you and your happiness until you graduate and move away for college. Then I will be able to think about myself while still worrying about you."

"I know. You need to not worry about me. You've raised me well and I make good decisions."

"But...."

"Mom. I know. I'm not going into drama, and I will take a stage name if I do theatrical productions. You have to be honest with someone and share our secrets. It's okay, and maybe we'd be a little safer if others knew. Zephyr is a small community, and they'll help us. I can feel it."

"That doesn't help when you've gone away to school."

"But if you open up and let others in—like Mr. DeSalvo—they can take care of *you* while I'm watching out for myself."

Dinah waved her off. "You don't need to worry about me. Taking care of myself is something I've done for over two decades."

"I know you can, but you don't have to—and that's the whole point. I guess I'll deal with the grief if you decide to get involved with Mr. DeSalvo before I graduate. But, for the love of Rodgers and Hammerstein, no PDA in school, okay?" She grinned.

Faith's a mini-me. She looks just like I did, only she's got her father's blonde hair. Dinah's stomach knotted. She smoothed over her expression, hoping she conveyed the absurdity of the conversation with her daughter. "I'm not foolish, Faith. The likelihood of something happening between Arlan and myself is slim to none. You said it yourself—he's hot. He's probably a flirt. It means nothing." *And it wouldn't be ethical to date my daughter's teacher, anyway.*

"But you don't know that. If something happens, let it." Faith's soft look melted Dinah's resistance. "Mom. Please."

"Go do your homework. You start dress rehearsals next week for your play and you need to be ahead, if possible. You know how those performances sap your energy."

. . .

ALONE WITH HER THOUGHTS, Dinah's purple gel pen floated over the multiple-choice tests her students had completed during her fifth hour class. She crossed out incorrect responses and left tallying until the end, giving her brain time to wander.

Images of Arlan's crooked smile and his chipped ceramic mug fluttered through her mind. *I should replace that for him. Maybe sneak a new cup into his classroom and leave it on his desk while he's in drama rehearsal.*

Arlan was taking over for Kelly McCoy—one of the English teachers, in her last year before retirement—who started off as the faculty advisor for the play. He'd been going to rehearsals and getting to know the students, the tech available and how it worked, as well as understanding the intricacies of a 300-seat theater, but the students mostly ran the show.

After she finished her grading, she wandered into the kitchen and made her nightly hot chocolate. She called out, "You want a cup tonight?"

Thumping from down the hallway grew closer and closer.

"Hell, yes. *Gilmore Girls* or *Charmed*?"

Every night they were home together, Dinah and Faith watched an episode from one series or the other. Dinah sipped her cocoa, and sometimes Faith joined her—other times, Faith went with chamomile tea and honey—particularly important to her during theatrical dress rehearsals and performances.

The ritual began when Faith entered middle school—when she started having questions about sex, relationships, and social issues, Dinah was glad her daughter trusted her enough to discuss them.

Homemade cocoa bomb, homemade marshmallow—both custom-created to fit the mug. These are some of the things I'll miss when Faith goes away to college.

Dinah blinked away the burn of tears as the DVD player opened.

"You pick," Dinah called, like she did every night. It didn't matter—except *Gilmore Girls* meant potential for serious discussion while *Charmed* provided the opportunity for light-hearted banter.

The *Charmed* intro music started. Dinah picked up the mugs and smiled.

"So, which episode are we watching tonight?" she said as she crossed the foyer and entered the living room.

"We're on episode three, season two, on our rewatch, so I thought we'd keep going."

Nothing specific tonight. "Perfect. I love rewatching in order."

Faith glanced at her. "I know." She grabbed the afghan from the back of the couch and curled herself into the overstuffed leather cushions.

As she did every night, Dinah set the mugs on the stone coasters on the coffee table in front of them. Then she settled into the other end of the sofa. She shared the blanket with Faith.

The pair sat in silence as Prue—one of the main characters in *Charmed*—admired a painting at an auction house and then read the words that appeared in the painting, sucking her into another dimension.

"What artwork would you like to get sucked into?" Faith asked.

"Ooh. That's a hard one. First, though, I wouldn't want to go anywhere without you, or be able to hop into a painting where you are." Dinah glanced at Faith.

Her brow creased, and then she grinned. "What if Mr. DeSalvo was in your painting? What type of scene would you want it to be?"

Dinah shook her head and sipped her cooling cocoa.

Mid-way through the episode, Dinah said, "A three-season porch, sipping lemonade. You can always get to know a person when you have quiet time alone with them. I think that'd be a wonderful way to get to know Arlan a little better."

"So, invite him over. Duh. It's not like the other teachers are clamoring over one another to be nice to him. This *is* Zephyr, and outsiders have to earn trust. I'm sure you remember how it was—still is, to an extent."

Zephyr had cliques, that was certain. But Dinah got out of the town what she put into it—which wasn't much. She didn't take part in the planning of the fall Harvest Festival, nor the Winter Carnival. She didn't work on the committees for the Spring Fling Extravaganza or the Summer Picnic.

She'd attended with Faith every year since their arrival. The events were fun and the whole community turned out for them.

"Is it really, though? Don't you get along well with all your classmates?"

"I mean, I do—but there're the kids descended from the council families that mostly stick to themselves. There are other cliques, too. Like any school. The council group seems to be the hardest to get into—as in, no one is allowed unless they could inherit a council seat. And, that same group is the school elite, too—they fill the student council and other positions of perceived power."

"But you managed to get some rather good roles in the school productions and even coauthored the play this year. That was your idea."

Faith rolled her eyes. "Mom, they know where their personal talents lie. They want things to be the best they can be and let others fill 'worker bee' roles—not leadership roles. That's why we don't have leadership positions in our clubs. The student council voted against it and sit as an advisory panel over all clubs. There're uniform bylaws for clubs that we have to follow. Big reason I'm not involved in anything extracurricular except drama."

"I guess I never realized..." Dinah took another sip from her cocoa before she continued, "Do you wish you'd grown up somewhere else?"

Faith shook her head. "Oh, hell no. Even though we're outsiders—and most of them call us that—I love our life in Zephyr. But I'm looking forward to being on my own in a couple years. Even if it's only dorm life at college."

A rock formed in the pit of Dinah's stomach. *There's so much we need to talk about. I think I should make a plan to tell her the whole truth about her father.*

HER EYES CHANGE COLOR. *Today, they're cobalt.*

Dinah's sexy sashay as she sauntered down the hallway in front of him captured his attention. It had been almost a week since she'd brought coffee to his classroom, and he hadn't seen much of her. She turned down the hallway leading to the art wing as Arlan and Janae proceeded toward the library.

"…but I don't think we'll have to completely revise the plan for AP courses," Ms. Brown said.

Shaking himself, Arlan turned toward his boss and said, "Whatever needs to be done, I'll get on it as soon as the play is over." He smiled.

Janae arched a brow and paused in the middle of the hall. "You have no damn idea what I said, do you."

"Busted. I, uh, am just a little overwhelmed with catching up on the *Midsummer Night's Dream* production and trying to keep up with all the new teacher things—including writing curricula for the courses I'm teaching." *I hope that was convincing.*

Janae shook her head. "I don't know you well enough to tell whether you're lying or telling the truth. Either way, I understand what you said, and I hear you. The first few years in a new role are typically the worst. It gets better." She started moving toward the library door and nodded as a slow grin spread across her face. The principal paused and said, "And I'm willing to bet you were *not* preoccupied with everything you have to do. But trust me when I say that Dinah is a sweet woman, and you could do worse—especially here in Zephyr—but don't you dare do a thing to hurt her if she lets you in. She's not dated anyone since coming here months before Faith's birth."

Unsure what to say, Arlan faced forward and said, "Thanks for the information."

Even though he wasn't looking at Janae, he'd guess her eyebrow was almost in her hairline, she arched it with so much dramatic effect. She said, "Let me know if there's anything I can do to help with your workload. And about the play? Just be an adult present—the kids can run the show without you, this time. They worked on it all summer and have done a fantastic job. It's been amazing supervising most of their rehearsals since July—when Kelly announced her retirement and inability to further volunteer—and it's magnificent."

She paused and took a deep breath. "Which reminds me. Since school's started, I'm much too busy to go to rehearsals any longer. Are you okay on your own?"

Arlan exhaled. "It's been great having you there, introducing me to the students and parents that pop in to help with set design and costuming the past couple weeks. I think I can handle it from here."

Janae stepped in front of him and entered the library. "Good. Now, I hope the principal has her shit together, so this doesn't take all damn day," she said, then giggled.

Arlan followed and rolled his eyes. "Right? It's not like we don't have papers to grade and lessons to plan or anything."

Then Janae waved at him and put her tablet on the circulation desk.

Arlan looked for a place to sit. The room was pretty full, and groups sat in cliques around the library tables. *The adults aren't any better than the students.*

Way in the back, a few seats remained open at a table, and he made a beeline. Just as he arrived and reached to slide a chair out, Dinah and Mara appeared.

"Oh. Hi. Is this your table? I didn't know where else to sit—no one…."

"You're fine," Mara said, waving him off with a paint-covered hand. She shoved a riot of curls away from her face before pulling out the seat farthest away from him, forcing Dinah into the empty area between.

"Yup," Dinah said, "The more the merrier back here. It's been Mara and me for so long, it'll be nice to have someone else that's a newcomer to talk with."

Puzzled, Arlan said, "But haven't you been here since Faith was little?" *Shit. Oh, shit. I shouldn't have said that.*

Dinah darted a glance toward Mara, who shook her head. Then Dinah sighed. "I've been here for almost seventeen years, but it doesn't mean I fit in." She glanced around, as though she were trying to note who might be listening. "I'm happy to chat with you about it another time." She smiled, a tight upturning of her lips that did not reach her eyes. She set a water bottle on the table then slid a notebook onto the surface, tipping over her beverage.

Arlan reached out to catch the container and righted it —without even touching it. *There must be some weird atmospheric thing here.*

"Oh, thanks so much for catching that. Clumsy of me," Dinah said.

Just then, Ms. Brown called the meeting to order and Arlan sat in tortured silence next to Dinah for the better part of an hour.

Their bodies were less than six inches from one another.

It was almost unbearable; patchouli and lavender and vanilla all mixed up into the most beautiful bouquet he'd ever experienced.

"She's going to call on one of us to say something about our favorite memory from the past week, so have something ready," Dinah whispered, her peppermint-scented breath dancing around his sideburns and tickling his ear.

He glanced at her, smiled, and nodded. *She's sweet. Seems like she'd do anything to help someone. And was that an invitation? Her "talk about it another time" comment?*

"Mr. DeSalvo, as our newest teacher, what's your favorite memory from this week?"

Mara chuckled.

"I'm not sure I'm the right person to ask, because I think everything that's happened since the first day of school has been magical. The students are amazing and are so kind and focused on ensuring everyone in the class succeeds—it's much different from the schools where I did fieldwork and subbing." Arlan glanced at Dinah and her smile made him melt.

"Thanks, Arlan. Glad to hear our strategic planning initiative is alive and well—we sometimes don't see it because we've been immersed for so long," Principal Brown said.

Dinah leaned over to whisper in his ear, again, "Great observation. Is it that bad outside our little bubble?"

Arlan nodded. "But let's talk about it another time."

She smiled. "Deal." This time, the grin he'd come to love appeared; her eyes sparkled, and she almost glowed.

When the meeting ended and staff began to disperse, Mara said, "I have some things to wrap up in the studio. Got some items in the kiln and need to make sure it switches off before I go for the day. You two kids have fun!" She giggled and waggled her fingers in a wave as her gauzy skirt fluttered behind her and she left the room in a flourish.

Dinah shook her head. "I swear, Mara is going to work herself to death. She's here until all hours of the night, sometimes. You know that kiln won't switch off until at least ten o'clock—she could leave and come back or ask our maintenance staff to check on it. But nooooooo. It has to be her doing it herself."

"Sounds like she likes to see things through to the end." Arlan shrugged. "Nothing wrong with that."

Dinah stood and picked up her notebook and empty coffee mug. "Are you leaving?" She glanced at his full bag as he slid into his chair, then hers.

"I am. I'd rather grade at my place than inside my classroom." He slung one strap of his backpack over his shoulder.

"Well, then. I should let you get going. I need to stop in my room and pack my grading and lesson plan book. Reflections don't write themselves!"

Arlan's heart pounded ferociously—like it might beat right out of his chest. *Walk with her. Talk about drama— her daughter is into it.* "So, um, this production of *Midsummer Night's Dream*. Have you seen many of the rehearsals? I have to return for a dress rehearsal run. The way they do drama later here—so athletes can participate? I think that's pretty cool, and great for the program."

Dinah nodded, her face beaming. "Faith cowrote the screenplay...which you know." The sexiest blush he'd ever seen crept up her neck and pinked her cheeks. "I saw a lot of the content as it was being written. They've continued to do modifications as they've gone through rehearsals to ensure it's as authentic of a modern retelling as possible. I also supervised many practices when Kelly and Janae couldn't make it, both before and after Kelly announced her retirement—it made sense since I was a teacher and Faith would be there, anyway."

Arlan nodded and followed as Dinah headed out of the

library in the direction of the history wing—which was the opposite direction from staff parking. "Is there anything I need to know? Tonight will be my first time attending a rehearsal by myself. Janae has been there until now. I plan to blend into the woodwork most of the time. She's been letting them take care of things, mostly."

She glanced at him but continued moving toward her classroom. A soft smile parted her lips. "I was planning to attend. Janae mentioned she couldn't make it in passing."

Arlan released a breath he hadn't realized he'd been holding. "That would be amazing. Seriously, thank you so much. I don't know whether the kids are behaving extremely well because Janae's there or whether they're actually like that."

"They're all very well-behaved because their parents have consequences for them if they're not. The town council whole-heartedly supports our behavioral expectations and has made them part of the town's mission."

They walked, side-by-side, the remaining yards to her classroom and he followed her inside.

Her teaching space suited her—she had painted the walls a pale lavender and had purple accessories throughout the classroom. Bulletin boards had shades of purple, and the draperies she had over transom windows along one wall were purple canvas. Gray, purple, and black rugs softened the gray-speckled industrial linoleum square tiles.

The room was tidy, and the scent of cleaning products —fresh, germ-free aromas—reached his nose. There wasn't a speck of paper on the floor, either. A small bag of trash sat next to the door.

"Tell me your secret, wise one," he said.

"What?"

"Your classroom is spotless, and I know they haven't come around to do any cleaning yet."

"Oh. That. The last few minutes of each class period, students pick up stuff on the floor around them, wipe their desks with anti-bacterial and anti-viral wipes, and straighten the classroom. My final class of the day also does trash and empties the pencil sharpener—and once a week they shake the rugs. They self-govern these activities in the classroom. The first week, I am the supervisor, but after that, they take turns in the position. You have to let them know what you expect, model how they might do the task, and they figure it out." She packed her things while she talked. "Maintenance mops weekly unless there's a need—otherwise, they don't even come in."

She grabbed the handles of her canvas tote, which stated, "History has its eyes on you," with the *Hamilton* logo and Lin-Manuel Miranda's image as the titular character. Then she walked through the space, moving a stapler on a table and a marker on the whiteboard chalk rail without much thought.

Arlan stepped outside the classroom as she neared the door, and Dinah stooped to pick up the bag of trash, which she deposited in the hallway. She then turned to make sure the door was closed and locked.

"If the trash is outside, they don't bother to open the door." She slung her tote over her shoulder. "Ready?"

Her smile brightened the sun-drenched hallway even more.

"Sure thing. Do you need to stop anywhere on your way out?"

She shook her head.

"Mind if I walk with you?"

She giggled. "Well, you've followed me from the staff meeting, so you might as well walk with me to the parking lot."

Heat crept up his neck, across his cheekbones, and over his scalp. "Yes. Uh, sorry if I'm being creepy. You and Ms. Slade are the only two teachers, so far, that have gone out of their way to make me feel welcome. "

Her face fell. "I'm so sorry, Arlan—I didn't mean it that way. Also, people around here keep to themselves until you earn their trust. It'll get better once they see you are an excellent teacher." Her fingertips grazed his forearm.

Electrical impulses arced between them—even after Dinah broke the physical connection. She paused in the middle of the hallway for a moment, then reached into her pocket and pulled out her phone.

"Uh, I have to...."

Faith turned the corner. "Oh, hi Mr. DeSalvo. I'm super excited for you to see dress rehearsal tonight!" She vibrated with excitement. "We've worked so hard on this production and think it does a great job tying the themes of the original to modern-day situations."

Arlan grinned. "I can't wait. As a matter of fact, I was telling your mom how I was nervous, and she's agreed to come along."

Faith's smile transformed into something extra bright and welcoming as she glanced at her mom. "That's great! Say, there isn't a whole lot of time before rehearsal, and we're only running home to grab a bite, then heading back here. You should come with us."

Looking at Dinah, he said, "That's the best offer—and the only offer—I've had all week."

chapter three

Horrified at her daughter's invitation, Dinah took a deep breath before she chanced a glance in Arlan's direction.

Is he blushing?

"I, uh, wouldn't want to, um, you know, impose or anything, though," he managed to eke out.

"Oh, you wouldn't be imposing," Dinah said. "I have plenty planned—mostly in case Mara decides to leave early enough for dinner, but it doesn't seem like that'll happen tonight." The fluttering in her stomach distracted her for a moment. "Please, join us. I don't know why I didn't think about it sooner."

"That would be great. Thanks. I do want to go home and change my clothes, though. I'm very much over this shirt and tie, and jeans will be more comfortable for a long evening of rehearsal."

"That's totally fine, Mr. DeSalvo. Whenever—it'll take some time for dinner to cook, anyway. Mom's marinating chicken in her special recipe and it takes around forty minutes to bake," Faith said, before looking at her mom and allowing a wide, mischievous grin to split her face.

The trio made it to the exit doors and burst into the warm fall afternoon. Distant sounds of whistles and football helmets and pads crashing against one another echoed. A pack of athletes jogged the edge of the property and parking lot as they warmed up for practice. A man took a net bag full of soccer balls from his SUV and slung them over his shoulder as he crossed their path to greetings of, "Hey, Coach," and "What's going on, Coach?"

Arlan's hair flamed in the sunlight. The red tone stood out and illuminated the kelly-green shade of the frames of his glasses. His beard and mustache framed his ruby lips and drew her attention.

"Mom. Let's go. I want to finish up my math homework for tomorrow before dinner."

"Oh, uh, yes. Sorry. Just enjoying the sunshine." Dinah broke away from where she'd rooted to the sidewalk, staring at Arlan. "We'll see you when you get there," she said over her shoulder.

"Um, Dinah?" Arlan said.

She stopped in the middle of the parking lot and turned toward him.

He closed the space between them. "I don't know your address." His sheepish grin was the most adorable thing she'd seen in years.

"Right. I forget what it's like to be new here. Everyone knows where someone lives as soon as there's a change made."

"Uh, I put all the staff members' cell numbers in my phone. Can I text you and then you can send me your address?"

Faith said, "I think she's got your number. She adds them when they're sent out."

"Well—"

"I'll have Faith send it once we get to the car." Dinah smiled and said, "It's comforting for me to know I can reach other teachers if I have a question, and don't have to wait for them to check email."

Arlan stopped at a black Prius. "Exactly. I'll see you in a bit, then. Thanks for the dinner invite." He put his bag in the back seat and folded his long legs into the hybrid.

A few spaces away, Dinah and Faith climbed into their Equinox SUV. Dinah dropped her phone in the cup holder and Faith picked it up.

"Don't send it right away—I don't want to seem too eager or anything," Dinah said as she pulled out of the parking spot and made her way to the street.

Faith sighed. "You told him you'd do it, or rather, that I would. Don't worry so much."

"I'm not worried, but I do think you may have over-stepped back there," Dinah said.

"Yes—I probably did, but you never would have invited him to dinner on your own. So, you're welcome." Faith went into the refrain from the "You're Welcome" song the Rock sang in that Disney movie.

Dinah thought about it. *Would I ever have asked him over? And what am I going to do now that I've—or rather, Faith—invited him?*

Upon arriving home, their large tabby cat with white socks, Mac, scampered underfoot the minute they entered the house, as usual.

Mac followed them from room to room as if to say,

"Good! You're finally here. Scratch my ears and entertain me, human."

Dinah had set her bag in a dining room chair and her phone on the table before she went to her room and changed out of her work clothes—capris and a T-shirt with a zip-up hoodie was more her style and much more comfortable. Upon returning to the kitchen, her cell started to vibrate.

I hope he's not calling to cancel....

Mac sat on the table—even though he knew damn well he wasn't supposed to—and swatted the device to the floor.

"Damn it, Mac. Stop it." Dinah retrieved the phone and swiped to answer. "Hello?"

"Hey, Dinah."

"Hey, there. Having a problem finding the place?" she asked.

"No, no. I haven't left yet. Was wondering whether wine with dinner would be appropriate? Just a glass, maybe? We could finish after rehearsal—"

"Ooh. I don't think so—not before. And I usually don't drink during the week. I'm afraid I'm a bit old-fashioned."

He laughed. "You're not old-fashioned. We'll have to revisit drinks on a Friday sometime soon."

Just then, Mac yowled. An attention-seeking move, if she'd ever seen one.

"Was that your—"

"Yes. That's Machiavelli—Mac for short. He's very demanding and hates to share his people. You should be ready to pay penance when you arrive." Dinah chuckled.

"I'll have you know, I'm a cat whisperer. Mac'll be eating out of my hand by the end of dinner."

"I don't know about that, but feel free to try. Faith may video him attacking your shins for no reason and text it around to her friends."

Arlan was quiet for a moment and then cleared his throat. "Are you sure there isn't something I can bring? I hate to show up empty-handed. My mom raised me to be a gracious guest and to always arrive at a lady's home bearing gifts."

Her breath stuck in her lungs.

After a pregnant pause, she exhaled and sputtered out, "We have everything. How about you come up with an icebreaker for us to do over dinner? That'll ward off silence and awkwardness."

"Excellent idea. I think I've got the perfect game. See you soon." Arlan disconnected the call.

Dinah put her phone on the table again and turned toward the refrigerator. After opening the door, she pulled out the marinating chicken—six breasts, plenty for a guest, plus leftovers for a few lunch salads.

Her thoughts drifted to Arlan as she went about preparing the poultry on autopilot. His hair, close-cropped at the sides and longer at the top, shone like polished copper in the sunlight. His beard and mustache—slightly darker; almost brick—glistened as though each strand held a dewdrop at the end. And the way his fair skin turned a brilliant red when he averted his gaze and then peered up.

Did he catch me blushing?

The way his lips pursed when he looked at her; like he fought back deliciously dirty thoughts.

She pulled out some fresh green beans and leftover crumbled bacon and set about preparing those to roast.

Must add garlic—that'll make me self-conscious enough to not want to kiss him—or even stay too close.

Her ruminations drifted back to Arlan, and she imagined him wearing the perfect cut of jeans which formed to his muscular tush and thighs. And then she imagined how tight his butt felt.

She transferred the beans, bacon, and garlic tossed in olive oil and parmesan cheese—as well as other spices—to a baking tray.

Just as well. What would a young man like Arlan want to do with an old lady like me? He's only being polite because he's lonely and people in Zephyr take a while to warm up to newcomers.

That was true—it had taken a long time for Dinah to have a sense of belonging in Zephyr. Even though she'd arrived four months before Faith was born, she hadn't made any friends and had no one to support her during the birth. She remembered the pointed looks of pity from the nurses when they came into the room as she labored.

"Honey, where is your man? Or even a friend? Are you all alone here?" the matronly nurse, who was around her age, had asked.

"I'm afraid so. I hope it's not too much trouble for me to be doing this myself," she'd said.

The woman had shaken her head and clucked her tongue.

"Don't you worry about a thing now. Hannah Arbruster's got you. We thought you'd have someone come in to help you before the little one arrived, or we'd have bothered you sooner." She'd grasped Dinah's hand, giving it a tight squeeze. "You don't have anyone—but now you're one of us. That loner shit ends today." And then she grinned. "I have a little girl—Kennedy—who is four months old. Your baby will be fast friends with her."

Mac galloped from the kitchen to the foyer, bringing her back from her memory. He sat at the door and howled.

Who needs a dog—

"Mr. DeSalvo is here," Faith singsonged from down the hallway of the ranch home.

Dinah shook her head. *That child will be the death of me, I swear.* "Thanks for announcing our guest, Mac," she said as she approached the door.

With her hand on the knob, she paused, took a deep breath, and smiled before swinging the door open wide. "Hey. You made it. C'mon in."

"I'M NOT sure what you used for a marinade, but I'm going to need the recipe," Arlan said as he wiped the corners of his mouth with the dark blue cloth napkin that had been tucked beneath the edge of his plate.

Dinah grinned. "It's really easy, but you'll want to have fresh garlic. That makes all the difference."

"And the olive oil needs to be extra virgin. Mom ferments her own apple cider vinegar, too. She uses it in the marinade—so don't let her tell you it's easy. It's easy for her because she's been doing this for so long that it's second nature," Faith added.

"It's not hard to make the cider vinegar—I always have a batch going, it seems. I can give you a jar—" Dinah started.

"I'd love to compare recipes and techniques, sometime. I make my own ACV, too," Arlan said.

Dinah's eyes opened wide, and she was...something. Impressed? Shocked? He couldn't tell.

Faith cleared her throat. "I'm...going to finish my math homework unless *someone* wants to give me the answers."

Arlan glanced away from Dinah and caught Faith's toothy grin. "I mean, I could do that, but you wouldn't learn anything that way." He shrugged.

Faith sighed. "Just as well. I need the practice problems so I can ace the test—whenever you're going to have that." She squinted her eyes, and her face shifted a little.

"Oh. You want the scoop on the test, huh? Well, if you must know, I'd planned to send home an open-book, open-notes test early next week. First one of the year, and first time you've taken one of my tests—only fair I give you a fighting chance to pass while you're learning my style."

Faith's expression softened. "Okay, then. As long as you're reasonable, that's fine, and I'll stop bugging you." She put her plate, silverware, and glass in the dishwasher before exiting the kitchen and calling out, "I'll be in my room, with the door closed, doing homework in case anyone wanted to kiss or anything."

Arlan glanced toward Dinah and then looked anywhere but at her. Heat crept up his neck and inched out from the edge of his beard.

Time slowed and stretched. Dinah fidgeted and started to speak before reconsidering a half dozen times. But a minute or less later, based on the digits on the microwave, Arlan found a way to get past Faith's comment.

"Teenagers, huh?" he said.

"I'm mortified, Arlan."

He looked at her and tears stuck to her lower lashes. "Hey, don't worry about it." He stood and extended his hand.

Dinah took it and he pulled her to standing.

Closing the distance between their bodies, until mere inches separated them, his gaze locked with hers. They moved together in a silent dance. The heavy air between them—thick with moisture—imprinted the memory of being close to Dinah in his flesh.

His eyes fluttered closed as he lowered his head, intending to taste her deep rose lips.

Mrrrrow!

Mac announced his presence as he walked between them, forcing them apart.

Cockblocked by a cat.

"Mac! Your timing sucks," Dinah said. She squeezed his hand and released him. "Why don't you explore a little and I'll clean up from dinner."

He reached for his plate. "No, let me help you."

She shook her head. "Really, it's fine. It'll only take a minute. Go see if there's any wildlife out back."

"You get wildlife?"

Dinah nodded. "About this time of day, we'll have some deer come in. Sometimes a fox or coyote will dart out of the woods—and I think I've seen a bear but scared it off when I called for Faith to come see."

"Okay. If you're sure. But when you come to my place for dinner, I'll be treating you like the queen you are." His gaze met hers once again.

She bit her lip in the sexy way that made his cock hard, so he turned and said, "Holler if I can help."

She exhaled a long, slow *shhhhh.*

The ranch-style house was arranged with a hallway down the middle and rooms off either side. The eat-in kitchen and living room were on one end—they took up around half of the length of the house—and the bedrooms and bathrooms were at the other.

He looked out the big bay window into the manicured backyard. Near the house, tidy flower beds with clusters of mums dappled yellows and burgundies through the dark, weedless mulch.

Mown grass gave way to the forest about fifty yards from the house. The edge of the woods was cleared of underbrush, from what he could see.

Faint music came from down the hallway, and he heard Faith singing to something he couldn't quite make out. Dishes clinked in the kitchen and Dinah hummed along. *I can't even make out what this song is, and they're synched.*

Arlan moved back into the kitchen.

Dinah stood at the sink, hands in dishwater.

He pursed his lips, fighting the urge to stride across the kitchen and wrap his arms around her from the back as he drew in the scent of her hair while pressing his body against her.

Instead, he stepped into the hallway, intending to find a bathroom.

The first door, on his left, had light hardwood floors, a large wrought-iron bed with a handmade quilt in soft pastels, and white lace curtains. The light and airy feel screamed Dinah—but what clinched it for him was the patchouli, lavender, and vanilla. A sense of déjà vu washed over him. *I've seen this room before. In my daydreams about Dinah.*

He closed his eyes and stood there, breathing in, and then exhaling out the tension and anxiety he'd allowed to build in his body. *This rehearsal got to me way more than it should have. Maybe it's not all about the rehearsal, though. I was nervous about coming here, but there's no reason for that. Faith seems cool about her teacher being here, and while I wasn't sure about Dinah's interest, I no longer have questions about that.*

Heat and pressure settled in the small of his back. He opened his eyes and looked into the backyard, viscerally knowing what would come next.

"It's so serene in here. I've made it a sanctuary. I read or journal a lot in this space. It's the only place in this house where I'm off-limits to everyone," Dinah said in a whisper.

Arlan stiffened. "I'm— I'm sorry. I shouldn't have been—"

Her hand stroked up and down his back. "No, no. I don't mind. If I were concerned about you seeing it, I would've closed the door."

Her hand found his, and she squeezed his fingers.

"Let me show you the rest of the house."

He turned to face her, and this time Mac kept his furry ass out of the way as he feathered a soft kiss against her lips.

Dinah froze with her eyes closed as she clenched his hand.

Arlan pulled back. "What? Did I fuck it up?"

Dinah smiled. "No. Not at all. Savoring the moment. A first kiss only happens once." She stepped into him, and her free hand slid up his chest and around his neck. She guided his head toward her waiting lips.

When they made contact this time, a dam of pent-up attraction let loose in his brain.

Dinah's mouth moved against his and her tongue swept the seam of his lips.

Arlan couldn't recall what happened for the next several minutes because all the blood in his body settled in his groin. But, when he regained his senses, he pulled Dinah against him, breaking their lip-lock.

He wanted her to know he wanted her.

He needed her to know that she excited him.

And he had to get a handle on his hormones before spending the evening at theater rehearsal.

It wouldn't be cool if students caught him kissing Ms. James in the wings. Not cool at all.

Tucked beneath his chin and wrapped in his arms, Dinah sighed and settled in as though she'd been in that exact position a million times.

"Perfect," she whispered as she slid her hand over his tush.

He smirked. "Running five miles a day."

She chuckled. "Not your ass. I mean, not *just* your ass

—it's pretty magnificent, though. You." She stepped back to look at his face. "This." She gestured back and forth between them. "Us. I think this could be perfect."

"That's a lot of pressure to put on something so early on, don't you think?" Arlan said.

Then, he caught a glimpse of the future—what the future could be. Having dinner together every night, arguing in the car about something intellectual on the way to work, attending Faith's college graduation— He saw it all as though it were happening that minute.

A lot like the way he'd pictured his first kiss with Dinah.

Dinah tipped her head to the side. "For right now, it's perfect. I know it won't always be that way—if there's even a future. But I think I'd like to find out."

He pressed his lips to her forehead and inhaled her scent once more before stepping away. "How about a tour of the rest of the house? If we don't leave this room, I'm worried I'll ravish you—and that would be embarrassing for all of us."

Dinah blushed. "The day will come when I expect you to ravish me, Arlan. Today is not that day. But I'm hoping soon."

Yes, soon. In the meantime, controlling his hormones and cold showers would have to do.

chapter four

A s the students went through each scene in *A Midsummer Night's Dream* and nit-picked one another's performances, Dinah's respect for Faith and the other actors involved in the production grew.

"I can't believe they've done this on their own," she whispered.

"I'm in awe. This is an amazing adaptation. Faith cowrote the script?" Arlan asked.

Dinah nodded. "She spent the summer working with Anthony Newman. Once they got the first act on paper, they brought in Layla Timmons and Kennedy Armbruster —they're directing, but it's been fascinating watching the entire cast work as a unit."

Arlan shook his head. "Their portrayal is so mature. How they've captured the themes and given them a modern spin. I'm quite fond of how they've handled the group fleeing to the woods and the Puck character casting a spell so two fall in love with the same person—and I'm especially excited to see how they handle the Bottom character's ass head."

Dinah glanced at Arlan, smirking.

Arlan blushed.

Simultaneously, they said, "Ass head." Then they laughed.

Someone wearing a microphone cleared their throat. Loudly.

The pair quieted.

"Thanks, *Mom*. We hope we haven't interrupted the hilarity for the evening." Dinah couldn't tell for certain, as she and Arlan sat halfway back in the auditorium, but she was pretty confident Faith rolled her eyes.

"Sorry, honey!" Dinah called out.

Faith grinned. "See that it doesn't happen again, okay?"

Dinah gave her a thumbs up.

Arlan nudged her arm with his elbow. "We should make sure we keep the volume down."

Dinah nodded. *But it's so easy to laugh with him. Such a shame we have to be quiet.*

He continued, "However, it doesn't mean we can't talk later. That is, if Faith lets you." His shoulders shook in a silent chuckle.

Dinah bumped her shoulder against his. "She's not the boss of me."

Arlan looked at her. His right eyebrow hitched upward.

"Okay. She *is* the boss of me, but she's worth the hassle."

Faith paused on the stage and turned toward them, glaring.

Dinah waved with her pen in her hand and made a production of placing the nib on the pad of paper, ready to jot down any notes she and Arlan had for the troupe.

"She's all business, huh?" Arlan asked.

Dinah moved her head from side to side, then pressed a finger to her lips. "Shhh."

As Faith and Anthony's Hermia and Lysander came to life before them, the intensity of the emotion between the two characters, portrayed masterfully by Lexie Matrious and Marc Keen, was evident. They captured one another—and their audience—in intimate moments that built and evolved.

Riveted to the stage, Dinah almost forgot Arlan sat next to her.

He sighed and nodded at the end of the first act. "I'm not sure how Faith and Anthony did it, but this is better than the original—or any other version I've ever seen."

"Agreed," Dinah said. "Do you have notes? I— I don't. I can't think of anything that would improve it."

Arlan nodded again.

Kennedy and Layla spoke to their actors as the troupe drank water and snacked on something.

Faith called out, "Do you have notes?"

Arlan replied, "Not at this time. But I do want to say that I feel as though you've got a wonderful Act I in place, and I can't wait to see what the other three acts look like."

Faith beamed. "Thanks, Mr. DeSalvo. Mom?"

Dinah shook her head. "Not a thing. I felt like it was perfect and opening night will be amazing."

Anthony called back, "Thanks, Ms. James." He grinned and did a little victory dance—at least that's what Dinah thought it looked like.

"Our Helena and Demetrius seem to be pleased with how the rehearsal is going. It must be nerve-wracking to have your play on display for all to see," Arlan said, interrupting Dinah from her analysis of Faith's demeanor.

"Faith and Anthony are glad they were cast. They auditioned for those parts. Layla and Kennedy were amazing with the audition process. Janae supervised that herself—so she was sure things were done fairly."

"I know I'm new and don't know anyone—I can't imagine other students portraying these characters."

Dinah grinned. "Yes, they are pretty perfect up there."

Arlan shook his head. "I hope they don't peak before opening night."

Dinah gasped. "Don't you say that Arlan DeSalvo!"

She sensed his apprehension. *Aw, hell. I should let him know I was only kidding.* Dinah giggled. "You are the best target for teasing." Then she smiled.

Arlan's face lit up like a spotlight shone upon him. *Amazing.*

"How do you do that?" Dinah asked.

Arlan tipped his head and peered at her. "Do what?"

"Light up even a dark auditorium when you smile."

He blushed. Through the darkness, pink crept up his neck and cheeks. "I'm pretty sure it's only because I'm with you." He toed something imaginary on the floor. "And maybe it's merely a reflection of your brilliance."

"Mr. DeSalvo, you've got me blushing like a schoolgirl. I mean, I don't see the girls around here blushing as much as I have since I met you."

Arlan leaned in and whispered, "Why, Ms. James! If I didn't know better, I'd think you were flirting with me." His breath tickled.

Dinah giggled and turned toward him. "Takes a flirt to

know a flirt, Mr. DeSalvo." She arched an eyebrow, giving him a "What've you got to say to that, mister?" full-of-attitude look.

"Not confirming or denying," he responded, grinning from ear to ear.

The actors took their places for the second act and Dinah placed a finger against her lips in a silent *shhh* directed at Arlan.

The pair settled back into their seats as the next act started.

Thematically, they'd selected teenaged years to represent the fickleness of youth in the romantic farce trope, and instead of the juice of a flower being the catalyst for shifting interest, they used a cell phone app to deliver a subliminal message.

Instead of finding themselves in a forest, the characters found themselves in a replica of the Zephyr town square—a place where teens congregated and hung out during the warmer months. The welcoming space had seating and tables the youth could use for eating takeout, playing games, or even doing homework. Fairy lights illuminate the area in a soft glow.

Dinah leaned toward Arlan and whispered, "It's just like the town square at night."

"I've not seen it after sundown."

"The Fall Harvest Festival will happen in late-October. That'd be a great time for you to see it. Might be weird if you go there and there are only students and young adults hanging out. I mean, high school and early college-aged kids," Dinah said, and then gasped and put her hand over her mouth.

Arlan smiled. "I'm older than I look, you know. And my grandmother always said I was an 'old soul.'"

"Grandmothers are supposed to think things like that about you. They're part of the job description or something."

Arlan pressed a finger to her lips. "*Shhh.* Before we're scolded again."

Dinah longed to draw that slim digit into her mouth and maybe give it a little nip with her teeth. *But that's an activity for another time, and another place.*

WITH MERE HOURS prior to the curtain going up, Arlan went about the school day like any other. He visited Dinah's classroom with coffee a couple of times; she came to his for lunch, and they walked out together at the end of the day.

It's not like we had the doors closed and lights off when we were alone. Arlan rolled his eyes as he disconnected the call from his principal.

"Hi, Arlan. This is a rather difficult conversation to have, so please listen until I finish."

His throat tightened and his mouth parched. He managed to croak out, "Okay—but—"

Janae interrupted. "So, you need to know this isn't coming from me as a person, but me as an administrator. There have been a few community members who have called, concerned because they think you and Dinah are dating. They don't like that around here, but if the damn town council did anything to make people who aren't born and raised in Zephyr feel comfortable and able to connect to the legacies, this wouldn't be an issue." She paused and took a breath. "Now, I know you and Dinah like spending time together. I think it might be a good idea to minimize the moments alone during school hours and the visits to one another's classrooms. Eat lunch together, but with the other teachers or invite Mara or someone else if you can't people. Hell, ask me."

Arlan started, "That's—"

"I know. Fucking ridiculous. Now, as Dinah's friend, I wanted to tell you that I've never seen her happier, so let's find a way to make this work without pissing people off."

The more Arlan thought about it, the angrier he got. "At least it's me pissed off and not a person who can pressure Janae to fire me."

Even though he'd run that morning, Arlan needed to feel the pavement below his feet and the subtle jarring of his joints to think through his conversation with Janae, so he'd donned running gear—Saucony shoes and socks with some cheap mid-thigh shorts and an old hoodie from Cherry Fest in Traverse City. The late September weather in northern Michigan was unpredictable at best, and downright horrible with snow at its worst. The balmy upper-50s overcast afternoon proved perfect for working out his thoughts.

He chastised himself for agreeing to talk with Dinah about the situation and problem-solving with her. *I should've told Janae to call Dinah herself.* He grinned. *Dinah likely would've given Janae an earful. Some would pay to see that.*

His muscles went on autopilot as Fall Out Boy's "Centuries" started to play through his wireless earbuds.

His pace matched the beat of the song. Arlan had spent hours curating his running playlists for various intensities and patterns of interval training based on the speed of the songs in the list. This was his slow-and-easy run plan.

As the melody wound down, he resolved to call Dinah after he finished his five-mile route.

Five or six students waved at him from the sidewalk as he passed the Mystic Burger Diner; more clustered in the town square and appeared to laugh as he ran a loop around the paved clearing.

After he crossed in front of the town hall and the clinic, he turned just past the library and entered what served as a spacious subdivision in Zephyr.

Small homes lined both sides of the street with perfectly manicured lawns a modest distance apart on deep lots. Each residence looked to be similar in size and shape—although some had additions. Likely from the 1960s, most domiciles were brick and had large windows in what was the living room area.

As Arlan plodded down the pavement, his thoughts returned to Dinah and the moments they'd stolen during school hours.

Nothing questionable.

Nothing inappropriate.

Nothing that couldn't be considered platonic.

Except it wasn't.

Nothing about Dinah and Arlan was platonic, and thinking about her made his chest tight and his breathing more rapid than it should be for his pace. Even his heart rate read higher than usual on his fitness tracker. *This is typical. When someone is attracted to another human being, these are the physical manifestations. My pupils are likely wide when I see her, and I blush. My palms sweat, and sometimes my tongue is stuck on the roof of my mouth.*

"Normal and accepted, however, are two different things in Zephyr," Arlan mused as he turned down the last cul-de-sac on the northbound street to make his way back home.

"Fuck this," he said, a little louder than he should have. Arlan glanced around and faced the judgmental glare from a fifty-something Zephyr legacy. "Oh, sorry Mrs. Matrious. A little nervous about opening night."

Her expression softened, and she said, "Break a leg! That's what they say in the theater, right?"

Arlan grinned. "It certainly is ma'am. Thank you so much." He waved as he finished the loop and headed back to the larger road.

I need to stop worrying about this. Dinah will know what to do, and it'll be fun listening to her and Faith bitch about the legacies. Water—mist-like drops—left his fingertips. *That isn't possible...is it?*

Shaking his head, Arlan pushed the event to the back of his mind.

He chuckled. If Dinah had her way, legacies—people whose family descended from the town's founders—wouldn't have any sway in the town. She'd complained about them numerous times because they went as far as to attempt to dictate the curricula she taught in her class-room at one point.

Even though Arlan hadn't known Dinah long, it was evident that she knew what she was doing and telling her what to teach would be a bad idea. He imagined her ire as she blew off steam with Mara or Janae.

Friend Janae. Not principal, Janae.

Which was the reason Janae didn't talk to Dinah herself. She wouldn't have been able to hide her real thoughts as well—because Dinah would've called her out on them.

An alert sounded in his earbuds. "Text message from Dinah." He tapped the device in his ear to play it.

> Did you want to come over for dinner before heading to the theater? I've got sandwich fixings and have plenty. Homemade bread….

When prompted to reply, he said, "Yes."

> I think I'm too nervous to eat. Maybe after?

> I'd like that.

> People are talking about us. We can discuss later.

> Fuuuck. Legacies?

> Yup. Janae called.

Dinah *ha ha*ed his last text.

Arlan didn't feel like a comedian. His stomach did flips, and his intestines tied in knots.

This wasn't normal opening night jitters. It was more.

His relationship with Dinah hung in the balance. They both needed their jobs, and Dinah had made a life for herself and Faith.

If anything more came of the complaints, he'd have to be the one to leave Zephyr. After all, he was last to arrive and had only been in town a little more than a month. Nothing connected him to Zephyr—except Dinah and Faith.

Not one to toss around the *L*-word lightly, he admitted he had feelings for Dinah that were significant. If she disappeared from his life, he'd be sad.

No. Not sad. Wrecked.

He'd come to love spending time with her. The way her face lit up when Faith came into the room. How she sang as she chopped vegetables. The dance she did while washing dishes. Her grading playlist—which he'd adopted. The light touch of her hand on his arm when they chatted in public.

And the way she kissed? Curled his damn toes and made his cock hard every time.

She did nothing by half measures, either. When she kissed him, it was never a peck; she focused on Arlan, his mouth, and how his body took up space. And then she stepped into that space.

Arlan DeSalvo had never met anyone quite like Dinah James. Everything was better, brighter for him. Food was more flavorful. He appreciated music in a way he never had before. A walk in the woods turned into an experience in listening and observing.

No.

I'm not ready to let this end. We'll figure out a way to

sneak around like teenagers or a way to tell the legacies to mind their own damn business.

That's what Dinah would say. He was sure of it.

Now, he needed to convince himself that he was up for the battle—one where love *would* conquer all.

chapter five

After three performances—Friday night, plus a matinee and an evening performance on Saturday —Faith was ready to sleep in and Dinah and Arlan made plans for a rendezvous.

With the striking of the set to happen later in the day, they arranged for Mara to supervise. And it was Mara's favorite part of every play—taking apart the pieces and visualizing ways to make them fit together for other productions.

With a sweatshirt, a cooler with several bottles of water, and a to-go cup of coffee, Dinah backed out of her driveway and headed west toward Petoskey after sending Arlan a text.

I am on my way. Stained Cup Coffee Company at 9 AM?

Um, how about going a little farther. I was looking on a map and Zorn Park in Harbor-something might give us more privacy.

> Do you want to meet somewhere and ride from Petoskey to Harbor Springs together?

Sure, that sounds excellent. It looks like it's a bit of a drive to Harbor Springs. Where do you want to meet?

> There's a strip mall next to the Stained Cup—let's meet there. Park near the pharmacy on the south end.

Got it. See you in 20 minutes.

On the long, isolated road out of Zephyr, leaves danced the flamenco on the trees, waving with their brilliant colors dancing in the sunlight. The rich reds and oranges on the maples contrasted with the dull yellows on the birch. Interspersed with pines of various species, the color palette, and the excitement of seeing Arlan jostled something loose that Dinah had forgotten.

"You certainly wear those jeans well."

Mickey Malone, a distant memory, demolished the solid walls she'd constructed to keep him from taking more from her than he already had.

Her stomach churned as his words blasted into her consciousness like the Kool-Aid Man on a sweltering summer day.

"And daaaaammn, girl. You want a burger to go with that shake?"

He'd never been elegant. Moving with clumsy steps through space, Mickey was always in the "find out" phase of "fuck around and find out"—and it had made her sweat —built heaviness within her, like someone had added one more brick to the weight crushing down on her.

"I'll have *my* dessert before dinner, thankyou-verymuch."

The day she'd conceded to marry him was much like that day. The sun shone and warmed her face as they'd walked along paths on Belle Isle, near his Joseph Berry Subdivision home, and she held a brilliant maple leaf, threaded with crimson, reds, oranges, and gold—the colors all swirling on the surface.

"I'm not going to have my kid be another bastard born into my family. That stops here—I will not perpetuate this."

"It's not only your decision, now, is it? I can't believe you have such an archaic perspective."

He slid his arm around her waist and drew her close, palming her flat belly with his other hand.

"It's an easy call, babe. I love you, and you are mine.

There's no escaping it. We're tied together for eternity and with this little bundle of joy on the way, it tethers us in one more way."

She broke out in a cold sweat.

"I'm not sure why you're balking at getting married. I can give you everything—the condo's paid for and it's in a building with security. I know the owner and it'll stay that way. I can hire a nanny and you can paint all day. It'd be a win-win—c'mon, you know you want to say yes." He released her from his grasp and jogged several yards ahead of her, turned around, and dropped to one knee in front of the fountain.

A photographer and videographer appeared, pointing their devices at her.

The *click-click-click* of the digital shutter on the camera made her heart beat faster. *Or is it the fact that Mickey is on one knee and there's no way I'm saying "yes" to him.*

"Regina Fontaine, will you do me the honor of being my bride? I promise to take care of you for the rest of your life and give you everything you deserve. You are the sun that brightens my days, and the moon illuminating my nights. Marry me." He held up a large emerald-cut diamond solitaire.

The videographer took a step closer to them.

The photographer snapped photo after photo.

Strangers stopped, gawking.

They're all waiting for me to say "yes"—it's the expectation. But I won't cave to societal norms. I can take care of myself, and this child, and I don't need a man in my life to do that.

"Baby? Whadda ya say?" Mickey's lips pressed together in a thin line and his jaw clenched and unclenched as he bit back more words.

"I don't know, Mickey. I think rushing into this is a little thoughtless and very unnecessary."

He popped up and forward, stepping into her space. His hot breath fanned across her face. Wintergreen. "I know you can do whatever you want—but I want to share this life with you. Don't you want to share yours with me? We have so much fun, and we practically live together now, anyway. There's no sense in renewing your lease since you're always at my place—"

"I'm at your place because you refuse to come to mine." She stomped her foot and ticked her chin upward a smidge.

Through gritted teeth, he growled, "Because your apartment is in a shitty part of town and my car would get jacked. Don't you think you're being unreasonable, baby? Can we try this again? And *really* think about your answer—there's a lot riding on it." Cruelty swept across his features and his eyes darkened from ice blue to cobalt.

She shuddered at the chill in his voice.

He wrapped his fingers around her upper arm and squeezed hard. Too hard.

She gasped and tried to wrench herself from his grasp.

His thick digits constricted her biceps more.

The pounding of her heart in her ears drowned out the ambient noise—no traffic, no birds, no murmuring conversations, no rushing water from the fountain. Her breath caught in her throat and couldn't pass a constriction in her airway.

I can't do this.

How will I escape from him?

He's never physically hurt me until now.

What will he do to a child that doesn't do what he wants?

What will he do to me if I don't cater to his every whim?

Is this what I want for me and my baby?

"No. I will not marry you." She pinned him with a steely stare, feigning confidence when her legs ached to carry her as far away from Mickey Malone as possible.

He dropped the ring.

The photographer and videographer lowered their cameras and inched away.

A stranger held up their phone, likely recording.

A feral grimace took over Mickey's face. With wild eyes, he spun around, making eye contact with the few passersby who remained. "What the fuck are you looking at? Get the hell out of here—" He lunged at the cell phone cameraperson, and they said little and turned, walking away as fast as their feet would carry them.

But they didn't go far. On the other side of the fountain, they sat on a bench and tried to make eye contact.

For a brief second, their eyes met before the stranger nodded their head and their eyes returned to their screen, thumbs flying.

"You're right, Mickey. You're always right." The

words stuck in her throat. "Let's try this again." She bit the inside of her lip to keep from screaming for someone to call the police—she needed to report the assault, retrieve her things from his house—but she sensed his common sense and logic had left the building.

His frantic pacing stopped. He approached her with slow steps, pausing to pick up the ring. "You mean it, baby? We'll be a real family?"

Be cool. Lie to him. You can do this.

"Yes. Let's do the proposal one more time—you've gone to all this trouble." She bunched her cheeks in an approximation of a smile.

The wild look in his eyes melted away. "You won't regret this. Now, make sure you act surprised, okay? I want to send this out as our engagement announcement. Maybe make it into a snazzy GIF or something." He licked his lips several times, his tell for uncertainty.

"Okay, Mickey." She glanced at the videographer and photographer.

Mickey turned to them. "Sorry about that false start. Do you think we can take it from the top?" He chuckled. "I've always wanted to be in a movie."

"Yes, sir. Give me a minute to..." Their eyes locked with hers.

She shook her head—a slight side-to-side motion —and their eyes widened before dipping their chin a smidge.

"...uh, a minute to change batteries," the videographer finished.

The photographer piped in, "I'm ready whenever you are."

"Oh, and can you trash the first take?" Mickey stood a little taller, pinning each of them with the stare he used to make sure a server understood he wanted his steak rare. *Trot the cow through a warm room and then slaughter it. That's how I want it.*

His expression reminded her of the sneer worn by Hannibal Lecter as he spoke about liver, fava beans, and chianti.

The cell phone cameraperson had found her on social media.

The videographer had tracked down her email and connected her to the photographer.

And she'd said "yes" to placate him, keep him calm. Until she could escape.

Battered and bruised from a fist to the eye socket after he'd been served with the restraining order, she'd gone to the police and filed charges and had Mickey Malone arrested.

But his slimy ass managed to get word to his "associates," and they delivered a message to her.

"Listen, Regina. I like you, but I need to do what the boss says." Regret shone across his pinched expression. He sighed and raked his fingers through his thick, inky hair.

She'd always liked Gunnar. He had picked her up from work a few times and gone with her to get art supplies. He didn't make her sit in the back seat if he knew where Mickey was—and there was no chance he'd be caught being too familiar with Regina.

She captured his gaze. "Do what you have to, but then?" She glanced around. "Get the fuck out of here and leave me alone." Barely moving her head from side to side, she bit her lip.

Gunnar nodded. "Thanks for understanding. Officially, I need to tell you to drop the charges against Mickey or you won't have to worry about the pain of childbirth."

She gasped, wrapping her arms to protect her unborn child.

Agony washed over Gunnar, and he appeared to swallow down something.

"Message received. What am I supposed to do after dropping the charges?" There had to be more.

Gunnar looked at the ceiling, blinked a few times, and sighed. "You're supposed to move all your stuff in here and get ready to go to the courthouse to get a marriage license as soon as Mickey is released." He looked anywhere but at Regina.

She gave him a quizzical look and scratched her ear.

Gunnar nodded.

His house is bugged.

She swiped at her eye with exaggerated movements.

Gunnar shook his head and mouthed, "front door."

Regina nodded—there was a camera outside the entryway. "Well, I guess that's that. Thank you for letting me know, and I'll be prepared for Mickey's return."

That was a lifetime ago—Faith's lifetime. Regina Fontaine had been four months pregnant when Mickey dragged her to the courthouse for a marriage license and they returned three days later to have a judge marry them.

She became Dinah James three months later.

But how do I tell the man I love that I'm still married to my abusive baby daddy and that I'm living under an assumed name?

HER EQUINOX SAT at the far end of the lot and Dinah's head rested on her forearms, draped over the steering wheel.

She's breathing. I wonder what's going on.

When the stressor of the legacies complaining about their relationship came up, she'd shown him her square breathing mantras:

- I deserve happiness.
- I am worthy of good things.
- I am my own person.
- I am safe.

Arlan pulled up alongside her and she startled, looking around panic-stricken. He waved and smiled.

Moments later, she sat next to him in the Prius.

Patchouli and lavender filled the car. Her trademark scent had a hint of spice, too—maybe sandalwood?

They'll take your man card for knowing that.

They looked into one another's eyes for a moment. But in that time, emotions surged through him, connecting him to Dinah in a way he hadn't thought possible before.

They drifted together over the center console, and he reached out his right hand to cup her cheek.

Dinah's fingers danced at the collar of his T-shirt until her palm rested over his heart.

When their lips touched, sensations he'd never experienced coursed through his body and washed over him when Dinah sighed and gave in to the passion between them.

They floated apart and Dinah's eyes fluttered open. "Hi." A soft smile spread across her face, and he sensed her calmness extending from her and wrapping around him like a fluffy blanket.

"Hi, baby." He laced their digits and drew her hand toward him, kissing her knuckles.

She sighed again.

"How was your drive?" he asked.

"It was...fine." Her expression shuttered, and she closed off part of herself from him.

Puzzled, he asked, "Are you sure? You seem...off."

"Thinking about the past. We do need to have a serious conversation—and soon. But can we not do that today, please?" Weariness played at the corner of her eyes and the way she held her mouth.

"So, what is there to do in Harbor Springs?" Arlan asked as he turned and put the car in reverse, backing out of the parking spot.

"You've not been there?"

Arlan shook his head. "I've been meaning to get out there, but when I arrived in town, there was this super nice history teacher that made me feel like going alone wasn't as appealing."

He glanced at her.

A blush crept up Dinah's chest and neck and settled on her cheeks.

"I love it when you blush." Arlan wiggled in his seat, adjusting his position as his cock grew hard.

"I'm— I'm not used to this type of attention, Arlan."

"Well, you better adjust. Because I don't intend to stop, no matter what the legacies say."

Dinah gasped. "I'd forgotten about that."

"Got a call from Janae on Friday. Before the curtain went up. Super shitty timing if you ask me."

She placed her hand on top of his and applied pressure, breath hitching inward without release.

"Breathe, baby." Arlan flipped his hand over and laced his fingers with hers.

Dinah exhaled, slowing her breaths, and her breathing returned to normal. "Thanks." She squeezed his hand. "Now, what's this about Janae?"

An expelling of air, slow and whistling, escaped through Arlan's lips. "Legacy kids. They've been complaining to their parents and Janae thinks we need to not be seen alone on school property. She suggested we sit together in the teachers' lounge or have Mara join us if we're not up to peopling."

"Wha—" she huffed out a sigh, then pulled her hand from his and took a drink of water. "Sorry, I can't react with anything except incredulity. What the actual fuck!"

"I reread my contract. There's nothing in it that says I can't be involved with another teacher—it has a morals clause. If I were to do something immoral, I could be dismissed. I feel like we could push back on this if you want to. We aren't even kissing or holding hands when we're on school property."

"Why the hell didn't Janae call *me*?"

Arlan chuckled. "I get the sense that she feels this is bullshit, just like we do."

"Oh, I'm sure she does. I'm surprised she's in the role she's in. I was certain they would promote Bert Matrious straight up to high school principal from middle school assistant principal, because Janae isn't a legacy."

"How is Bert a legacy?" Arlan asked.

"His mom—Marjorie—is on the council. Bert will take her seat eventually."

"So, tell me more about this town council and the legacies—and how all that works."

"I can't believe we haven't gone through this yet!"

"Why? We're getting to know each other and that is way more important than some assholes whose families have lived in Zephyr for more than a couple of centuries."

"That's absolutely true. And I, for one, am grateful you're here and you're interested in me." She smiled, and the animosity about the whole legacy situation evaporated.

"Still, I kind of need to know what I'm up against...."

"It's *us*. *We're* up against the town council and their vision for the town. At times, I feel like they really don't want anyone new in town—that they want to keep Zephyr like a gated community—where the only newcomers are invited in after thorough vetting."

He chuckled. "For real. That's *exactly* how it was for me."

"It was?" she asked. "How so?"

"I applied for the job, posted through Grand Valley's alumni portal, and when I heard back from Sochi Nauk, they wanted to have a pre-first-interview session with a council member. They were willing to come to me, and we met at a local coffee shop. They asked questions about my values and beliefs, how I grew up and was raised. It was... weird. I asked why they needed so much ancient history before I would be approved for an interview with the school staff. Nate Armbruster, who came for the 'interrogation,' said they're cautious about who they invite into the community and want to ensure each new person is a good fit for their values—which includes understanding the importance of the celebrations the town has and their belief in living in harmony." Arlan shrugged. "I like learning about other cultures and that kind of thing, so I was cool with it."

"Huh. When I applied for my job and moved here, it wasn't quite so rigorous. Maybe their perspective has changed. Like they're being pickier."

"Well, in this post-COVID world, you can't be too careful with who you associate with and let into your life. One of the questions they asked was my stance on vaccination—naturally, I am all for them."

"Oh, the council was extremely strict about leaving Zephyr during the COVID lockdown period. It was rather nice to not have to worry too much about people coming in and out and possibly bringing the virus back—anyone who left the town limits had to quarantine for ten days and have a negative COVID test to return to masked participation in indoor events for a very long time. Now —I'm sure you've noticed—people still mask indoors often. Anytime they've traveled a lot or been in a risky situation, they monitor, test, and mask. For example, I would have opted to sit outside over indoors—one reason I chose the Stained Cup, because they have a cute patio with propane heaters—and I would have masked when inside. If we'd had to sit inside due to the weather, I would have tested and masked. There are a lot of older legacies in town, and we all take protecting them from the virus seriously."

"It's a condition of my continued employment—vaccinating and the testing you're talking about." He glanced at Dinah.

She nodded. "They had us all sign an addendum to our contracts about it. As far as I know, not one person balked."

"See, this is one reason I find it so weird that you and Mara were the only friendly teachers who were willing to reach out to the newbie, who was also new to the area."

"Oh, that's easy. Most of the others are from legacy families, married into them, or are good friends with them."

Something at the edge of his thoughts sloshed and surged before disappearing. "It seems these legacy families are in charge around here. What's a person gotta do to get *in* with them?"

"Well, Nate Armbruster is like a father figure to me and a grandfather to Faith. Olivia babysat Faith when I went back to work and continued to do so until my young hellion started school. The Armbruster family took us under their wing when Hannah—Kennedy's mom—found out I was here by myself. I know them—they're good people."

Dinah sighed. "I do, however, think some of the council members are mired in the past and what *was* instead of being appreciative of what *now* brings. Although, I'm not sold on the fact that they're stuck in the days of yesteryear— as you know, we're very accepting of LGBTQIA2S+ people and center some of our education on it. I teach about the Stonewall Inn and about Black trans activists—who started the movement of Pride parades and demonstrations."

"I've noticed the students are open and accepting, but not so much the adults. This whole thing about teachers 'being involved' isn't welcoming—especially in a small town."

"I know. That *is* strange. And I've never heard of something like this happening before. Then again," she sighed, "this is an unusual situation that's not happened during my tenure at the school."

"I hate to ask this, but I want us to be transparent with one another. Is this a deal-breaker for you?"

She laced her fingers with his again. "Absolutely not. I'm up for the battle if you are. And I'm willing to do whatever Janae says to ensure the council is happy."

"I think it's better that we don't mention this to Faith. She's well-respected and has a lot of friends and I don't want this to color the way she views the legacies."

"I don't keep anything from Faith. She's old enough to make decisions on her own and needs to be aware of what is going on, should she decide to live in Zephyr after college." The steel in Dinah's voice cut him to the core.

He squeezed her hand as they drove down M-119.

"You're right, of course. I didn't realize you'd dealt with so much, living in Zephyr. It seems like you both know what's going on and have your finger on the pulse of the town."

Distance crept between them, and she withdrew her hand again to drink more water. "I think we have a temporary solution for this—can we abandon this topic for now, too?" she asked.

"Certainly. So, what's there to do in Harbor Springs?"

"There's the lighthouse. And some cute shops. We should be able to get a takeout lunch and eat at the park. There's a lot of history in the area, too. Shipping and tourism, mostly. There're a few historical markers there, and a few more we can stop to see on the way back." She chuckled. "Faith usually rolls her eyes and makes a fuss about stopping, but I can't get enough of 'em."

"I like learning historical facts—one of the ways we learn about the history and science of an area is to understand the natural resources, which is evident through documented events." He pulled her hand toward him and brushed her knuckles with his lips. "And what's even more captivating is doing it with you."

Arlan froze. "I mean, not *doing it* doing it—because I wouldn't know about that but learning history with you." The heat crept from his chest up his spine and over the top of his head, settling in his cheeks.

"Arlan, you don't have to be so careful about innuendo with me. We'll get there—hopefully sooner rather than later." She squeezed his hand.

"I don't want to rush you and fuck this up."

"Same. And, if I'm being truthful, I've wanted to take

you to bed for a long time." The breathiness of her voice stirred new feelings.

Raw, primal feelings he'd not felt for another person, ever. And with all the complications involvement with Dinah James brought into his life, he wouldn't want it any other way. "You know, I feel the same way. Just... I mean, I want it to be perfect. I don't want us to have to plan everything out, so we don't get 'caught' by legacies—and I don't want us to feel like we're sneaking around like a couple of teenagers. We're old enough to make our own decisions without the input of the council."

"Yes—I agree. And I want the same. It's important we're open with one another about where we are, what we're feeling. Because I don't want this to become some chore for you. And I don't want that for myself, either."

Settling their hands on Dinah's thigh, Arlan traced the subtle diagonals in the fabric of her jeans.

"Most importantly, I don't want to lose your friendship, Dinah. So, if you want to take this relationship to the next level, I'm all for that—but we need to be realistic about what it means if we decide it's not working."

"Oh, you won't be rid of me. I know firsthand how lonely it can be here without someone to hang out with or confide in. Mara knows some things, but not everything —" Dinah stiffened, and she glanced out the window.

"Hey, you said not today, so let's stick with that, okay?" He swept his thumb across her inner wrist.

"You're right." She turned toward him. "Today is for us and exploration."

Today, the magic will happen.

chapter six

Being with Arlan DeSalvo short-circuited her brain, at times. Like when his lips brushed against hers in an innocent kiss she wanted to be much, much more.

Like now. They made out in his Prius, next to her car, like a couple of teenagers learning the ropes of how the whole sex thing works. Hands over clothes, no touching aching private parts, and not talking about how turned on and wet Dinah was for Arlan.

And they didn't talk about his raging hard-on that likely would be the cause for a cold shower.

His tongue swiped inside her mouth, searching, exploring. And then he pulled away. "What the hell are we doing? We're two consenting adults. We shouldn't have to sneak around, making out in my car like we're doing something wrong."

"I was wondering when you'd get there. Plus, I'm not as flexible as I used to be, and this is giving me some serious aches." She chuckled, softening her comment, which was true—but she didn't want him to think she was in pain.

"Come to my house," Arlan said. "We'll drop your SUV off at your place. I park in the garage, so no busybody neighbors—unless they see you as we're driving in."

Her nipples peaked even more, and her eagerness to be alone with him in his private space increased. Where only the two of them mattered—without prying eyes and caution at the forefront. The ache at the apex of her thighs escalated, and she shifted in her seat, looking for a little relief.

Relief that didn't really come with the use of her vibrator.

"Yes. We'll be careful, so we aren't seen. I...can't wait." Her gaze flicked toward his crotch and back to his umber eyes, full of care and concern—and...maybe even love.

"I'm so glad you agree." His fingers skimmed down her neck, over her collarbone, and lingered at the swell of her breast on the way to her waist where they settled, and he squeezed.

She shifted in her seat again and sighed. "If you're serious, let's go. I can let Faith know the plan—well, for the car drop-off, anyway."

"Oh, Dinah. You have no idea how you affect me." His palm slid from her upper arm to her wrist and pulled at her hand, resting it in his lap, on the ridge of his erection.

Her breath caught in her chest and her clit throbbed—once, twice, three times—before she exhaled and smoothed her hand over his pants, eliciting a groan. "I'm not going further here—no need to get busted by the cops for indecent exposure. I'm sure that'd be a problem for our contracts."

He groaned and then chuckled. "You never fail to surprise me, baby. But one thing I know is that I can't wait to get you out of your clothes. All of me very much agrees."

Arlan's erection throbbed in time with her most sensitive nub—one part of her that had been neglected.

"I can tell—and I'm rather eager to feel your skin against mine. And for you to feel how you affect me. It's so hard to adequately describe because these are things I haven't felt in— Well, things I've *never* felt."

"Let's go." He cupped her cheek again and their lips met in a soft, sensual kiss full of promise and satisfaction.

Dinah pulled away, regretting the decision as her fingertips itched to explore Arlan's body. Her parts longed for his touch—his caresses and his kisses—even more than she longed to bring him pleasure.

She gathered her belongings.

Arlan sighed and put his palm over his erection, squeezing. "I can't wait to explore your body and make you feel good."

Heat settled in her cheeks and her intimate parts flamed. Her tongue swept across her lips. "Arlan, you're killing me, here. Let's go, already." Her thighs pressed together.

"See you at your place. I'm not planning to get out of the car and open the door for you, in case Faith is there, watching, or any neighbors are. They don't get to see what you do to me." His eyes were hard, with an edge she'd not seen before. Full of protection for her, them.

Mist emerged from his index finger and swirled around her in the vehicle. Dinah blinked. *What was that?*

"Did you see that?" she asked Arlan.

"See what?"

He'll think you're seeing things. She shrugged. "Never mind—it was probably dust motes caught in sunlight."

"Or maybe it's the magic between us," he murmured.

A smile broke across her face. "That's it." Her hand rested on the door handle—her exit would drop her into reality for a brief time.

"I'll follow you," he said, and leaned toward her.

She met him and a kiss full of need and the promise of satisfaction exploded within her.

Tap-tap-tap.

They jumped.

Outside the driver's side window, stood a police officer. He gave the motion for Arlan to roll down the window.

Switching on the vehicle, Arlan lowered the glass. "Hello, sir. What can I do for you?" He smiled.

"You folks have been sitting here for a while. Why don't you take it somewhere more private before I need to write you up for indecent exposure?"

Arlan blushed and nodded. "Thanks, sir. We'll do just that."

The officer's deep brown eyes locked on Dinah's. "Ma'am. You have a good day now."

"Thank you, sir." *Don't ask for our ID. Don't ask for our ID....*

He pinned his focus on Arlan, then nodded. "Let's not meet again under these circumstances. Understood?"

"Loud and clear." Arlan smiled.

The cop walked away, and Arlan rolled up the window.

"You heard the man. We'll need to make sure we're not making out in the car anymore."

They burst into laughter at the same time.

"That could've been grounds for dismissal if we'd been written up," Dinah said.

He chuckled. "Right, but if I'm honest, I wouldn't trade this for anything. Now I've got a reason for you to come to my place."

She bristled momentarily before she peered at him. "We can be alone at my house. Faith's not there every single minute I am." And then she smiled. "She's even dropped hints about leaving and doing stuff with her friends if we want some 'adult time.' Even went as far as asking what our 'signal' would be—like in *Friends* when Chandler and Joey work out the necktie thing."

Arlan cackled. "So, what's the signal?"

Dinah rolled her eyes. "We don't have one because I am a responsible parent and Faith isn't my bestie."

He shook his head. "No, Mara is."

She pinned him with a stare. "Actually, you are. And that's what I need in a relationship—I need to be friends with someone before I can be intimate with them."

"Let's get going—so we can have some of that physical intimacy." He paused, glanced out the window. "You know I'm really...in *like* with you, right? Because that's something *I* need—even if it sounds old-fashioned."

When he faced her, his plaintive expression and the hope in his eyes tugged at her heartstrings. "I'm in *strong like* with you, too." She opened the door and then turned back to Arlan. "I think *we* have potential—and I'm not just saying that to get in your pants." She got out of the car and shut the door.

Arlan rolled down the window. "Good—because I'm not in the habit of making out with women and then not following through. I definitely want us to see where this thing goes, Dinah. Wherever it leads."

She nodded, emotion clogging her throat, and got in the Equinox.

Me, too. Arlan. Me, too.

I CAN'T BELIEVE *she's in my house. I never thought this day would arrive.*

"You've got more furniture than I thought you'd have, for a bachelor just coming out of college."

"Well, I'm a couple years out of school, now—the last one I spent student teaching, and I subbed full time for most of another year."

Dinah's expression dampened. "I keep forgetting that you're so young. You seem like such an old soul."

Arlan stepped toward her and drew her into his body, fusing them together from chest to knee. His erection pressed into the soft round of her belly, below her navel.

She shifted from side to side, sliding her thigh around one of his and pressing her womanhood against his leg.

"Age is a number. And it doesn't matter to me what that number is, as long as we're both in agreement about where we are about *us*."

She tilted her pelvis and ground against him, her hipbone along his cock. Then she looked up at him, her eyes fierce. "I'm all in, Arlan. And I'm not willing to sacrifice my happiness—or yours—for anything."

After a beat, their lips met in an intense, bruising mash. With probing tongues and roaming hands, the kiss deepened and additional need, want crept in—making their movements urgent.

They separated and Dinah reached for his waistband, fingers opening his fly and shoving his jeans down his hips to release his hard dick. She gasped. "Oh, Arlan." She licked her lips and began to lower herself to her knees.

He grasped her upper arms, keeping her from her intent. "Not a chance. Not our first time—I'm not going to last because I've wanted this since the moment I first set eyes on you."

"But— I, uh, have..." Dinah's expression fell.

"Oh! I know I'd love your mouth on my cock. I know I'll come too fast. And while I recover pretty quickly, I want our first time to be one we'll both remember for all the right reasons. So, that means I need to make sure you're as close to the edge as I am." He slipped a palm beneath her T-shirt, and then another, smoothing over her soft skin as he lifted the worn cotton up her body and over her head.

Her breasts, encased in a satin bra, pressed together, creating cleavage he'd one day slide his dick into. *But not today.*

Dinah unbuttoned her skinny jeans and shimmied out of them, standing before him in matching satin panties curving over her ample ass in a way that made him even harder.

Letting his pants and boxer briefs fall to the floor, he stepped out of them and peeled off his ancient Rolling Stones T-shirt. "Can I see all of you?"

She blushed, whispering, "If that's what you want."

"Dinah," he tilted her chin up with his index finger,

capturing her eyes with his, "if you're not there, that's okay. If it's too fast—"

"Not at all. I, uh, haven't ever been with someone who wanted to put me first." She averted her gaze, looking over his shoulder. "I think I have a little baggage from my younger days around my body and sex."

He kissed her cheek, nuzzling toward her ear. His soft exhale brushed past the shell, moving her hair. "Your body is beautiful, Dinah. Anyone who said otherwise is an imbecile. Let me show you how it should be, baby."

A shuddering breath left her, and she smiled as a single tear trailed down her cheek. "I trust you, Arlan. Show me —show me how to love you."

"We're not worrying about me. Because you being here and trusting me with this part of you is all I need."

She stepped into his embrace and grabbed his ass, pulling him toward her, his erection pressed against her smooth skin.

He ground against her once, eliciting a moan from her lips.

"Let me love you, Dinah."

"Okay."

Arlan moved back, laced his fingers with hers, and led her to his bedroom. "Will you climb into my bed?"

She nodded, sitting on the edge and scooting to the middle before pivoting. "Is here...."

"That's perfect. Now, can I take off your bra?"

She nodded.

Arlan crept up her body, kissing his way from her left ankle all the way to her left ear. He propped his chin up with one hand while the other slid over her ribs to the center of her back.

Dinah leaned toward him, giving him easier access to the clasp, which he opened with a flick of his fingers. The bra sailed behind him without a second thought.

She shifted to her back, and he perched above her, with one thigh between her legs, against her satin-covered mound. He kissed her nose and then plundered her mouth again before tonguing the shell of her right ear, nibbling down her neck, and circling her rosy areola before he pulled it between his lips.

The weight of her breasts in his palms was exquisite, and he pinched her other nipple as he sucked and nibbled her dusky peak.

She arched into his ministrations, caressing his forearms, and raking her fingers through his hair, occasionally gently tugging the strands.

He dragged his fingertips down her torso to her mound, where he pressed the heel of his hand.

Rising to meet the pressure, Dinah ground against his thigh. Arousal dampened her panties.

After plundering her mouth again, Arlan murmured, "Your body is magnificent." He sat up on his knees to her side and hooked his index fingers into the sides of her undies and tugged them over her hips, down her legs, and off her toes, smoothing his hands against her skin.

Dinah wrapped her fingers around his engorged member while the sight of her pussy mesmerized him.

Her touch almost undid him. Arlan placed his hand over hers. "Not this time—I'm barely containing myself as it is."

She released her grasp and slid her palm down his thigh. "Soon, then. Very soon." Her soft smile, not quite reaching her eyes, shone in the afternoon light.

Shifting to settle between her thighs, Arlan kissed the roundness below Dinah's navel and each of her hip bones. Her trimmed curls and scent drew him in.

She peered down her body at him, an unreadable expression on her face.

"Let me taste you, Dinah." He slipped a finger between her lips, teasing her entrance.

She shifted her hips, inviting his digit into her slick warmth. "Oh, god, yes."

With one swipe of his pointed tongue, he licked from her entrance to her clit and circled the sensitive nub.

"Oh, yes. Arlan, don't stop."

He groaned, his tongue still against her. Then, laved her bud as he inserted the tip of one finger.

Her thighs trembled around his shoulders and her breathing quickened.

Slipping his finger deeper, he curled his digit upward, and she rewarded him with a low moan.

"Oh, yes." Her hands trailed from his head to her breasts, and she cupped them in her palms while manipulating her nipples, pinching, rolling.

"Come for me, Dinah. Tell me how to get you there."

"Oh, don't stop. Keep doing that—and put your mouth on my clit."

"You got it." Smiling, he settled in, alternating between flicking his tongue and sucking on her sensitive nub, with a few nips for variety.

He added another finger, stretching her slick walls and increasing the pressure against her G-spot.

Clasping her thighs against the side of his head, muscles in her passage fluttered against his fingers and her clit throbbed against his tongue.

A low moan, from the depths of Dinah's being, broke past her lips as Arlan focused on her pleasure and tipping her over the edge, into oblivion.

Shuddering, the pitch of her utterance rose and then she stifled it, pressing her lips together and internalizing the sound that almost caused Arlan to explode along with her, tight between her thighs, he stilled his tongue and fingers, allowing her to ride out her orgasm.

Once she lay motionless and her muscles relaxed, allowing her thighs to drop, Arlan sat up and wiped her essence from his beard. "You okay?"

She smiled and nodded. "You're pretty good at that."

Arlan grinned. "If you were impressed by that, wait until you see what's next." He settled next to her, pinning his erection along her hip. "But first, I want to hold you."

"Oh, no you don't." She propped herself up on one elbow, looking around. "Where are the condoms?"

He rolled toward the edge of the king-sized bed and reached into the top drawer of the nightstand, pulling out a strip of three. He set them on the pillow as he rolled back toward her. "That should be enough for now."

With an arched brow, she said through a smirk, "I hope so. It's...been a while for me."

"Baby, when you're done for today, just let me know."

Chuckling seductively, Dinah said, "Where do you want me? I want you inside me. Now."

His penis twitched, eager to find itself in her tight, wet sheath. "I think I need to control this time, or I may embarrass myself."

She reached for the condoms, tearing one off the strip, and ripping the foil packet open.

"Um, including this part. Your fingers on my dick right

now would not be a good idea." He took the condom from her, grasping the base of his cock and unrolling the prophylactic down his length in one smooth motion.

Dinah settled on her back, pillows tossed to the side as Arlan moved between her thighs, sliding the tip of his member against her slit.

"Are you ready, Dinah? I'm going to try to go slow and gentle—but you tell me if it's too much."

She nodded, eyes wide.

He kissed her and, as his tongue entered her mouth, his member breached her entrance.

"Oh, you feel so damn good."

"Yes—right there," Dinah declared as Arlan slid deeper inside her passage.

Noting his position, he pressed farther forward.

Dinah's legs wrapped around him, heels beneath his ass against the back of his thighs, holding him there. "This is— this is amazing."

"I am— shit. I need—" He withdrew to the point where she'd noted pleasure and stroked shallowly a few times before going deep, almost withdrawing, and then repeating the process. Then he palmed her breast and tongued her nipple to a hard peak, sucking it between his lips and flicking the tip.

She moaned again, her thighs tightening around him.

"Touch yourself—show me how to make you come while I'm inside you."

Dinah's gaze met his, unsure, questioning. "Are you sure? I've never— I've never done that with a partner before."

Leaving her breast, he laced his fingers in her hair and kissed her deeply while seating himself inside her, then released her mouth. "Then you've had some shitty lovers. You know your body best—show me how to pleasure you." He pressed his torso upward, hovering over her.

She grinned, slipping her hands over her breasts and playing with her nipples, before using one hand to spread her lips.

Arlan's cock twitched inside her as he looked at the place where they joined, and Dinah gasped.

She swept her index finger around his penis and slicked her juices on her swollen clitoris. "Move. Now. It won't take me long—especially if you do... Oh!"

He focused short strokes on the spot that drove her wild before going deep and almost withdrawing. Arlan repeated the pattern as she flicked her bean. He grasped and pulled her thighs for leverage.

Pressure built, and he tried to hold off—until....

Dinah pressed her finger against her nub and a low cry exploded from her lips—again, she stifled the sound, and it resounded in her chest as her silky walls quivered around him, drawing him deeper into her than he thought possible.

With one final stroke, Arlan buried himself, balls-deep, inside Dinah, and filled the condom with his release.

Collapsing on top of her, still connected, he rolled them to their sides and reveled in the shared moment.

chapter seven

Sweat trickled down her back—and it had nothing to do with heat, for a change.

As she made her way from the school office to her classroom, small pockets of students stopped talking as she approached, stared at her, and then turned and whispered to their friends while furtively glancing at her as she walked by.

Dinah was not surprised when she received Arlan's text.

Tell me you aren't catching students
whispering when they see you.

Shit.

💀 💀 💀

"Oh, Ms. Ja-ames!" Mara's sing-song voice floated down the corridor.

I wonder what she knows...I have a feeling I'm likely to find out.

Mara slipped her arm into Dinah's, and they walked shoulder-to-shoulder toward Dinah's classroom.

Mara shut the door behind them.

"The scuttlebutt is that you were at Arlan's on Sunday evening," she said, barely containing her glee. "Were you *checking papers* together?" She cackled.

"Mara!" Dinah feigned incredulity. "That's exactly what we were doing. Checking papers." She rolled her eyes. "And every busybody can keep their nose out of my business."

Tsk-tsk-tsk. Mara clicked her tongue while shaking her head. "You know the council isn't going to be happy. I'm surprised...."

The classroom door opened. Janae grinned as she stuck her head in the entryway. "Got room for one more?" She closed the door behind her.

Dinah sighed. "Give it to me straight, boss lady."

She crossed her arms over her chest and gave Dinah the stink-eye. "As your principal, I must remind you about the morality clause in Arlan's contract. It doesn't appear in yours, but if the council pitches enough of a fit, it'd be a justifiable suspension."

"Heard loud and clear," Dinah responded.

"That's horseshit, and you know it. Teachers are allowed to have personal lives. In a town as small as Zephyr, where do they expect those of us who are single to find partners?" Mara bit out.

Janae cleared her throat and put her hands on her hips. "Amen, sister. As your friend, I gotta know: How good was it?"

Mara cackled again.

Heat crept up Dinah's chest and neck, settling on her cheeks and continuing to rise. The roots of her hair flamed.

"Girl. *Girl*—I am not kidding when I say it's about damn time." Janae chortled and hugged Dinah. "I'm going to bat for you two—especially you, because the council loves you. But I need you to keep this on the down-low for a while. What I said to Arlan on Friday? Make sure you're always chaperoned on school grounds. And that heat between you two? Smother it during the school day. Geez, the sexual tension is so thick you can cut it with a freakin' knife."

Mara piped in. "Dinah, seriously. Let me know where you're having lunch and I'll hang out with you."

"Or sit together in the lounge—unless it'll be too hard to keep your hands to yourself." Janae chuckled again.

The warning bell rang, startling all three women.

"Well, let's get to work, ladies!" Janae said as she strode across the room and opened the door wide.

"See you at lunch," Mara said, squeezing her upper arm before exiting.

Her phone vibrated in her pocket. She pulled it out and looked at the sender. Faith.

Why didn't you tell me?

Tell you what?

That you went to Mr. DeSalvo's house on Sunday! I thought you just went somewhere together, like a park or something.

How did you find out?

I overheard. People aren't talking in front of me.

We're keeping things platonic at school, like we planned already. If someone asks, how will you handle it?

I'll tell them it's none of my business—or theirs. LOL.

Dinah "hearted" Faith's response and slid her phone back into her pocket.

First hour started off a little rocky—most of her students smirked at her until she decided to give them a pretest on the new material for the week instead of holding a discussion.

She asked questions and students responded on note-book paper.

"Ms. James? Isn't it a little old school to have us take a hand-written quiz?"

Dinah pinned Dot Reyer with a stare. "It's a skill you

need to maintain even though we're in the age of electronics. Plus, I decided last minute to make today's overview a pretest." She smiled. *Might as well get it out of the way.* "Any other questions?"

Melanie Hyland raised their hand. "Ms. James, you know we all care about you, right?"

Dinah's heart leapt into her throat. She nodded.

Melanie looked around the classroom.

The small group of seniors nodded back at them.

"You can't say you heard this from us, okay?"

"Understood. Go ahead."

"Some of our family members are on the council and they had a meeting last night about you and Mr. DeSalvo."

Ice ran through Dinah's veins. She eked out, "Okay...."

"We were talking this morning and decided you needed to know they met. We don't know whether they're in favor of your relationship or not. But..." they looked around again "we thought you should know so you can be, uh, maybe a little more discreet."

Dinah crossed her arms in front of her, weight resting on one leg. "I'm— I'm unsure what to do with that information but thank you for trusting me enough to spill the tea." Dinah grinned.

The students groaned collectively; most of them smiled.

"Seriously, though? Thanks." Tears welled in her waterline, and she blinked them away as she glanced at the clock. "We've got about ten minutes left. How 'bout I give you time to start tomorrow's reading?"

"Sounds good."

"That'd be amazing."

"Hell, yes."

Dinah moved to her desk with the pretests and sat down to check them as she made notes about what the students knew and areas where their collective knowledge was lacking.

The small group of fifteen seniors spoke to one another in hushed tones.

Natasha Garber checked their phone—something Dinah allowed during quiet work time as long as it was quick. They looked around, clearing their throat. "Um, Ms. James?"

Everyone centered their attention on Tasha.

"My mom said the council is going to push for a written reprimand in your files and strict guidelines both you and Mr. DeSalvo have to follow moving forward."

Students rolled their eyes and shook their heads, muttering variations of, "This is bullshit." "What business is it of theirs, anyway?" and, "Uptight assholes."

"Thanks for the warning." Dinah stood up straighter. "It really isn't anyone's business what goes on between two adults, and that's my stance on this issue."

"Oh, we agree one hundred percent, Ms. James. And don't worry. If anyone starts giving Faith or Mr. DeSalvo a hard time, they'll have to deal with us." Kennedy Armbruster's statement was backed by her standing in a legacy family.

"Faith is aware of the situation, thanks to overhearing classmates. What you might not know is that we're used to changing our behavior to suit the council and what's expected in Zephyr. It isn't easy to live here because we are strangers—even after almost seventeen years of living here." She looked at Kennedy. "Your family has been the most welcoming, but we still feel like there's a big secret no one is telling us."

A collective gasp filled the room, but the students glanced at each other uncomfortably.

"You can't be serious...."

"That's not what Zephyr is about...."

"Our families want people to feel like they belong...."

"I hear what you're saying," Dinah said, "but that's not how they're coming across. I just thought *you* should know. And I'm ashamed it's taken me so long to say anything."

"It shouldn't be necessary for you to say something, Ms. James. We should have been able to tell and should have gone to our families." Lexie looked around.

Students nodded.

"We're so sorry. We're going to do what we can to change things, moving forward. And if we can't get buy-in from our families, we'll strive toward making the changes ourselves when we get to the council. That would likely take a long time, though, so I'm really hoping they listen now."

Dinah nodded. "Because you've been candid with me, it's my turn. If things don't change, I'm prepared to leave Zephyr. I shouldn't have my personal life scrutinized and shouldn't have to keep my personal relationships a secret."

"Oh, we agree."

"Absolutely."

"I mean, Zephyr is a small town. Where are you supposed to meet people, if not at work?"

Marc interrupted. "Excuse me. This might not be as

simple as we think." He glanced around the room before focusing on Dinah again. "There are things you don't know about Zephyr, Ms. James. And it's not safe if we tell you."

"Shit," one student said under their breath.

"We all need you to be careful with who you trust and what you agree to—and please, don't ever mention this conversation. We'll all be in serious trouble if our families find out."

Her heart clenched in her chest and skipped a few beats as the ominous warning settled around her. "You've got my word. And I thank you."

The bell rang and Dinah positioned herself near the door, thanking each student as they left.

"Be sure you tell Mr. DeSalvo everything, okay? He needs to know. But no one else—not even Faith."

Thomas Stebbins' advice made the hair on the back of her neck stand on end. "Got it. And thanks again."

With her classroom empty, she sent Arlan a text.

> Let's talk on the phone after school. I'll have lunch in my room. You go to the lounge. We need to do damage control—at least for today.

Shit.

Yup.

"WHAT THE HELL, Janae? Are you telling me this

town council can tell me who to love—or rather, who I *can't* love?"

Janae's eyes sparkled with mischief. "Did you just say *love*, Arlan? Does Dinah know?"

Shit. "She does *not*, and I'd really, genuinely appreciate it if you didn't mention this to her. I suspect the feeling is mutual, and she senses it, but it's too new to say it."

"My lips are sealed." The spritely woman bubbled enthusiasm as she mimed turning a key in a lock near her mouth.

"Thanks. Now. Let's get back to 'what the hell' for a minute." Arlan pinned her with what he hoped was a stare so serious it'd tamp down some of the principal's eternal energy. "If the council decides one of us has to go, it'll definitely be me. Plus, Faith only has a couple more years of school, so it makes sense for Dinah to stay."

"We both know she'll insist on leaving, too. And Faith won't want to stay here if it means Dinah is unhappy. I have a feeling you'll leave together, if it comes down to that."

A surging undercurrent moved between them as Arlan crafted his next words. "What if I were to go before the council and plead our case?"

Janae chuckled, shaking her head. "That is ill-advised, my friend. They don't know you at all. At this point, you should wait for an invitation from them. Besides, Dinah already said she was going to the council. She's well-liked and accepted as part of the community. She'll have better luck getting them to accept your relationship—and has a very long-standing connection with the Armbruster family. Nate is like a grandfather to Faith." A grin spread across her face. "And if Dinah happens to mention that she's in…

In the *L*-word with you, well, that might make all the difference."

"So, I'm supposed to let Dinah handle it? Can I even go with her as moral support or to answer questions the council might have for me?

Her lips smashed in an uncharacteristic frown and her brows knit together. She tilted her head and stared at him hard, as if assessing him in some way. Like a switch flipping, her expression went from contemplative to excited. "I think everything will work out. You'll probably be called before the council, anyway—but let Dinah handle the relationship stuff."

"Why would the council summon me?" Arlan picked up his water bottle. The cool liquid inside sloshed along the wall against his palm. Each *slap* of the fluid against his hand settled him.

He stilled, focused on Janae. Her entire form shimmered in front of him, and for a second, he thought her skin was blue. *Just a trick of the light. Or maybe stress.*

Arlan grasped the bottle in both of his hands, preventing him from taking his anger out on an unsuspecting table or wall.

"Arlan—your water..." Janae's eyes grew wide, and a grin spread across her face.

Inside the bottle, the liquid swirled. The movement matched the way his panicked and stressed mind processed his frustration.

He set it on the desk and stepped away. "I— I wasn't doing that... Wasn't rotating the bottle to make the water do that."

Janae nodded. "It's okay. This is one of the reasons you'll need to see the council." She grasped his wrist and rubbed her thumb along the inside. "Don't worry about this one bit—it's actually a good thing and will help your case."

Jerking his arm from her grip, Arlan fumed. "What the fuck—er, sorry—but what are you talking about? There's got to be some weird geomagnetic force going on here in Zephyr. The water in my house seems to have a mind of its own at times, and I swear I can conjure a soft rain when it's really hot out and I'm running."

She smirked. "'Conjure' is a good word." Nodding, she took a step backward, toward the door. "Don't let your temper get the best of you—I have a newfound sense that things will work out for you and Dinah." Janae wiggled her fingers as she stepped out of his classroom and into the hallway. She pivoted sharply and strode down the hall until she caught up with a group of students and settled in with them, chit-chatting like they were besties.

Don't forget—you need to go to the lounge today for lunch. I'm sorry you have to do that.

Just had an interesting convo with JB— she doesn't seem as worried as she did before.

We'll talk more later.

He pulled his lunch out of the mini-fridge behind his desk and grabbed his water bottle before almost dropping it. *Nope. No more creepy water stuff.* Instead, he hooked a finger around the handle of his chipped green ceramic mug—the one his parents had given him when he graduated with his teaching certification.

"Arlie, I'm so proud of you. Even though you had to push through high school to get to a place where you could shine, you did it. And you're breaking the cycle. Your bio mom loved you so much. She gave you to your mom and me and we've spent our lives nurturing you in an effort to repay her for her trust in us and the true gift you are to the world. I know you're going to do remarkable things one day," his dad said as the three of them stood in the kitchen.

The ceramic cup had felt cool in his hands when his mom gave it to him.

"Your bio mom was still pregnant with you when she met with us. There was this cute little diner in Lansing—and we were happy to go anywhere to meet her. We'd talked on the phone and sent some letters and pictures. I slipped my empty coffee mug into my purse at the end of the meeting because I wanted a memento—something we could give you that was part of that memory for us." She smiled—it was full of warmth and love.

"She was hiding from her family. We offered to let her stay with us, but she said it'd be too dangerous. And she was terrified they'd find out she was pregnant, so we never got her full name. I don't even know if she gave us her real first name," his dad added.

"Why haven't you told me about this before now? I mean, this is important shit."

"Your mom wanted to tell you once you were eighteen. I thought you needed to be older because men's brains are a little slow." He chuckled.

"I appreciate that you both were so truthful with me about being adopted. I've never felt like I needed to find my birth mom or her family. And I still feel that way—but knowing she felt like she was in danger and hid to keep us safe? I kinda want to meet her someday." The ice cubes in Arlan's glass sitting on the counter rapidly melted, even though it was only sixty degrees outside and cool in the kitchen of his parents' house.

They'd kept the fifties vibe in the kitchen of the split-level floorplan, a cookie-cutter copy, layout-wise, of the houses on either side. Parts of Midland, Michigan had built up when Dow Chemical hit its stride after World War II when it diversified and became a household name.

"I'm afraid we don't have any contact information for you—and even though I took some calls from her in those early years, they stopped when you started school," his mom said.

Arlan put his hand over his mother's. "Thanks for telling me this part." He glanced at the cup. "I always wondered why you kept this on your dresser, but never asked. I wish I had, now." He smiled. "This cup is part of my history."

His dad nodded. "And I love the way your mom tells the story."

Arlan bit his lip, stifling the tears that burned his sinuses and threatened to spill down his cheeks. "She does. It's one of the reasons I'm so glad she is my mom." He pulled her into a tight embrace.

Arlan pushed back the chair and stood abruptly. He took the five steps across the eat-in kitchen to look out the window over the sink into the backyard.

His memory took him back to when he was young and playing on the splintery swings they'd built with the help of his uncles. Mom used to push him on the swing for hours—and when they went to the park, she'd run with him on the playscape and chase him down the slides and pretend to be the first mate of a ship at his side.

He'd had a good childhood and his parents had kept him safe—physically. Those school bullies were another story, but they'd gotten theirs during the sixth-grade end-of-year field trip to the water park. They'd been in the wave pool and were teasing Arlan because he was so skinny; to hide his thinness, he wore a T-shirt in the water instead of going shirtless. According to the lifeguard, they were caught by an undercurrent. The three of them were pulled under and held there for several minutes before they reappeared, spitting and sputtering. And Arlan, who stood next to them, wasn't affected at all. The boys had said Arlan pushed them, but his hands had been crossed over his chest the entire time—hiding himself from the world.

When they accused Arlan, he'd said he'd controlled the water—made it take them away from him.

Who knew they'd believe it? And when Arlan

had threatened to sic a tornado on them, they'd promised to never tell anyone his secret.

Arlan hadn't heard his father moving toward him. His hand rested on his shoulder. "I'm glad to see that smile—we've definitely had some good times back there."

He put his hand over his father's fingers, on his shoulder. "You two did a fantastic job raising me. I couldn't have asked for better parents." Turning, he added, "Now I've got to get things packed. I'm supposed to pick up the U-Haul tomorrow morning —incredibly early."

"I wish you were staying here. This house will seem so empty—" his mom stood and joined them. She sniffled.

"I'll be back to visit—and if a teaching position opens up here? I'll apply for it."

"I'll keep an eye out and let you know," his dad said.

Arlan nodded. "In the meantime, let's double-check those kitchen boxes and make sure I have everything I'll need—or have it on my shopping list. It'd suck to pull out a can of Spaghetti-Os and not have a can opener for my first dinner in the new place."

"You're not having Spaghetti-Os for your first meal in your new home!" his mother said.

"Have you been making me freezer meals behind my back?" Arlan asked as he turned to look at her.

She smirked. "Absolutely. And I'll keep doing that so I can bring you more when we visit you in the Motor City."

"I've got your recipes—I put them in a database so I can't lose them." Arlan laughed and pulled his mom in for a hug.

The next week, his mom had received her diagnosis: an aggressive form of uterine cancer. She died four days before his move to Zephyr and those early days were rough, but Arlan thought moving and new surroundings were better for him and allowed his dad to get on with his life instead of living in the past.

While she valiantly fought the disease, he'd come home almost every weekend. She'd wanted to sort through everything in the house—thirty-five years of memories—and get the stories written down. Sometimes, they voice or video recorded her reminiscing.

In his own world, the past drifted to the back of his mind and the teachers' lounge came into focus, the chatter between his colleagues becoming a tangible echo in his head, prominent among the other noises in the room, even though it shouldn't have been.

"...I heard the council is going to do something about them."

"...He's so much younger than she is—what does he even see in her?"

"...Oh, um, hey, Arlan!"

Silence settled over the room.

"Hey. Hear any good rumors?" He peered around the room, making periodic eye contact the other parties couldn't hold.

A few chuckled, uncomfortable.

"Yes, I know. Zephyr is a boring little town—*nothing*

exciting happens here." Picking up the empty container from his lunch, he stood, hooked a finger through the green ceramic cup's handle, and moved toward the coffee maker. After filling his cup, he said, "You all have a great afternoon," before whipping the door open and exiting into the silent hallway.

If only my mom could meet Dinah—she'd love her almost as much as I do.

chapter eight

He knows where we are. How the fuck did he find us? This can't be happening. This isn't real.

She locked her phone and then unlocked it again, the tremor in her hand making it difficult to tap the opening her messaging app. They were still there. *And still terrifying.*

They come in late in the afternoon, just before school let out. Dinah had checked them because she assumed it was Faith letting her know about after-school plans.

It wasn't.

"Ms. James? Are you okay? Is something wrong?" Annika Pope asked.

Startled from her shock, she said, "Oh, I'm fine—I

received an unexpected text." She tried to smile, but the effort hurt her cheeks.

She had never lied to her students and didn't intend to start. They knew they could ask her anything, and she'd provide an authentic response.

Scrutinizing her expression, Annika shook their head. "Whatever you say. Are you sure you're okay? I could go get Ms. Slade or find Faith...."

Dinah shook her head. "I'm fine—thanks for checking, though. That was quite thoughtful and perceptive of you." She glanced at the wall clock. "Last five minutes, humans. If everything is done, you've got free time."

Moving toward her desk, she took in her classroom, cataloging what she should take with her if she needed to leave town with Faith. *Absofuckinglutely nothing. All we need is each other and our memorabilia boxes.*

Dinah kept the box current with snapshots of the two of them and other keepsakes. Besides the "go" bag she always kept packed and in the back of her closet—rotating out clothes by season—it was the only thing they needed to take with them.

He's found us.

Faith didn't know a lot about her father—she'd asked when she was younger, but Dinah had kept her answers brief yet honest.

"He's a not-nice man, Faith. It's better that we're not around him."

"But Mo-om. What if I want to know him? You can't keep me from him forever."

She'd pinned tween Faith with an icy stare. "I can. He's dangerous, Faith." She sighed and softened. "Listen, I know it's hard to not have answers. It's better if you don't know—safer for us both, maybe even the entire town."

Faith froze. A moment passed. Then, "That bad?"

Dinah nodded and blinked away tears.

"Okay. I trust you. But one day you'll need to tell me."

That night, Faith had packed her own "go" bag and started keeping a box of mementos.

> Hey. Let's get a move on right after school.

We were going to debrief the play.

> Reschedule. We need to talk.

...

The dots appeared and disappeared several times.

I hope it's not....

> It is.

BRT

Leaving her laptop on her desk and a neat stack of checked papers next to it, Dinah pulled a few personal items from her drawers and put them in her bag. Chap-stick, a hairbrush, toothbrush, and her spare coffee cup. *Anything that might contain DNA.*

She glanced around the room. One student kept glancing toward her. Dinah took two deep breaths and tried to put on a soft smile. Hoping it worked, she approached the whiteboard, like she did every afternoon, and wrote out the agenda for the next day's classes. *Keep everything normal. Normal, normal, normal. Nothing to see here.*

The bell rang for end-of-day dismissal, and Dinah turned toward her students, sending them on their way with the usual well-wishes. "Don't forget to read the first section of chapter twelve!" she said a few times—so all had a good chance at hearing the reminder.

Normal, normal, normal. Nothing to see here.

"Have a good night, Ms. James. I hope everything's okay—you look really worried," Annika said.

Dinah touched their upper arm. "It's all fine, Annika. Thanks for your concern."

They paused, searching her face for something. "I'm not sure I believe you, but you've never lied to us before, so I suppose I should. Let my family know if there's anything they can help with—and I mean it, Ms. James."

"I'll reach out if we need anything. I promise," Dinah said, hoping her voice sounded sincere.

Annika nodded and left.

Moments later—which seemed like hours—Faith arrived, eyes wild and carrying a full backpack.

Dinah pulled her into a hug. "We've got this." She squeezed Faith tightly against her before releasing. "Do you have everything from your locker? Leave all your books?"

Faith nodded. "I have English homework, but it's reading *Frankenstein*, and it's my personal copy. Also, I have a math worksheet, but don't need my book to do it."

Dinah took her spare sweater off the back of her chair and stuffed it in her bag. Then, she opened the curricula binders for her courses and made sure the sticky notes were on the proper days so someone could jump right in and continue with her plan for her students.

"Mom. We gotta go. I can't keep my shit together much longer." She blinked and turned away.

"We've planned for this day. Everything is set. All I'll need to do is make a few calls as we head out of town." She left the part about ditching their cell phones unsaid.

Her heart ached and her throat grew tight. *Arlan.*

Outside the classroom for what Dinah thought might be the last time, she locked the door and pocketed her school keys. The plan was to leave them on the kitchen table and tell Janae she could get them to give to the sub.

The two women walked down the hall. Faith pretended to read something on her phone and Dinah hoped she looked as exhausted as she felt—and that it'd keep anyone from stopping them.

Safely in the Equinox, Faith said, "You need to call Mr. DeSalvo. We haven't talked about our plan since you met him. He needs to know. Vanishing wouldn't be cool at all."

Dinah nodded. "You're right. I was hoping it'd be okay with you. I know we've said that we were only going to tell Mara we had to leave."

"Mara knows what's going on a little bit. Arlan doesn't at all—does he?"

"He does not. I wanted to tell him on Sunday, but I didn't want to spoil our time together."

Faith snickered. "Everyone thinks you're doing it with him."

Dinah smiled. "And? We're both adults."

"Oh, definitely. You know the council. They can be a little...."

"Old-fashioned?"

"Let's go with that." Faith looked at her phone.

Dinah glanced toward her.

She scrolled through her camera roll, deleting images and sending a few to the home printer.

"Don't forget to make sure they're off your cloud. We can't leave behind any identifying pictures someone could find. It'll keep our friends safe."

Faith nodded and swiped at her nose with her oversized sweatshirt sleeve.

After backing into their driveway and situating the SUV as close to the side door as possible, Dinah glanced around before exiting the vehicle.

Once inside, they went in opposite directions, checking all doors and windows, ensuring the house was secure, and closing all window treatments. Then both went to their rooms, each bringing out their suitcase and box of memories.

Mac followed them from room to room, yowling because they hadn't scratched his ears yet.

"I'll bet Arlan will come get Mac. They get along well," Dinah said, choking on the emotion in the words. Mac had been with them since Faith was a toddler, but it wouldn't be fair to take him with them while they were running.

Faith picked up the fluffy feline, snuggling into his fur. "You're the best cat, Mac. I love you."

"I'm going to call Arlan—I'll be in my room. Stay away from the big windows." Dinah scratched Mac's ears before slipping into her room.

Can we FaceTime?

Just about home. You okay?

Not really.

I'm coming over.

This is a good idea—he can take Mac and my keys with him. That way, no one is in danger from coming into the house.

I'll be watching for you. Use the side door and park on the street near the neighbor's driveway.

Dinah, you're scaring me.

I'm terrified.

I'll be there in 2 minutes.

Sliding her phone into her back pocket, she sat on the edge of her bed, looking around the room as she inhaled and exhaled, using her breathwork.

With purpose and determination, she opened her nightstand drawer and pulled out the baby Glock and the full clip. After loading the firearm, she rose and left her bedroom.

"Hey, Mom—when is...." Faith's gaze centered on Dinah's right hand, where she held the gun. "When the fuck did you get that? Has it been here all along?" The wild look returned, and Mac jumped from her arms.

"Yes, I've always had it. It gave me a little peace of mind. I sometimes go to Mara's for target practice." Dinah moved through the house to the side door, located in the laundry room—where a garage would be if she'd ever had one built.

"I'll get Mac's food and treats together." Faith sniffled and turned away from Dinah. "I feel like there's so much you haven't told me, and everything is unraveling."

Dinah peered out the small window in the door and spotted Arlan walking up the driveway, looking around, paying attention to his surroundings.

He'll be okay after we're gone. There's no reason to believe Mickey would harm him—or anyone else—if we're not in Zephyr.

Unlocking the door, Dinah stepped outside with the gun ready to fire but pointed at the ground.

Arlan paused. "Babe...."

Dinah tipped her head toward the door. "Get inside. I'm right behind you."

"DINAH. WHAT THE HELL?" Arlan said once the door closed. "Are you in trouble with the law or something?"

She shook her head. "This is going to sound unbelievable, but we're hiding from Faith's sperm donor—my... husband."

"Again. Dinah. What the hell? And can you put that thing down?" He motioned at the weapon.

She glanced at her right hand and jumped a little—like she was startled that she held a firearm. "Certainly. Faith hates guns, too—but I've needed to have it just in case... and today is the day I need it."

Faith carried the bin of cat food and a box of treats and toys for Mac into the kitchen. "Hey, Mr. DeSalvo."

"Faith, I think you can call me Arlan when we're not in school."

"Thanks. Not like it matters much, now." Her puffy, red-rimmed eyes had a sheen of tears.

"What the hell is going on here?" Arlan asked.

Dinah chewed on her lower lip, then sighed. "Have you ever heard of Mickey Malone?"

Faith gasped. "*He's* my dad?"

He drew in a narrow column of air, as though through a coffee stir stick straw, and Dinah's response reached him muffled, like he'd plugged his ears with cotton balls.

"He is. One of the reasons I teach about him alongside Capone is to parallel the two. Mickey is no less dangerous than the mobster and has more technology at his disposal, making things exponentially more perilous."

"Fill me in—I haven't had the pleasure of taking one of your courses," Arlan said, shaking to clear his head, calm his thoughts.

"He's on the FBI's top ten most wanted list. They thought he was holed up somewhere in Detroit for a while but think he might be in Puerto Rico or even South America," Faith said.

Arlan pinned her with a stare.

"What? I keep up with these things. You know, lots of people are interested in 'True Crime' stories? This is how I fill that need," Faith said. "But he's my dad. Shit, I know why you didn't tell me now. Is it even safe for Arlan to know?"

Dinah took his hand. "Probably not, but knowing who to look for is half the battle. So, I think the benefit outweighs the risk." She looked at her feet, pressed her lips together, and took an audible deep breath. "My name isn't Dinah, either. It's Regina Fontaine—but I feel like that scared girl is gone now." She squeezed his fingers. "I love the person I've become. Moving to Zephyr was the reset button I needed. I've been able to give Faith a pretty normal childhood and"—tears welled along her lower lashes—"and I am so lucky to have fallen in love with you, Arlan. I wish the three of us could run away and start over, but that's not realistic." She sniffled and wiped the moisture away with the heel of her hand. Pressing her lips together again and taking one more deep breath, she said, "The biggest honor of my life—besides being Faith's mother—is being loved by you, even though we only had the chance to begin our journey."

He pulled her into his chest and held her as silent sobs wracked her frame.

"Um, can you take Mac? He likes you—well, at least he doesn't attack you," Faith said with a chuckle.

Arlan nodded his head. "Absolutely—but what if I *do* go with you?" He stepped back and tilted Dinah's chin up and looked into her eyes. "Nothing's holding me here." *Except you.* Ripples made his fingertips tingle.

"I can't be responsible for you, too. It's enough to keep

Faith safe." Dinah cut a glance toward her daughter. "And...what if something happened to you? I could never forgive myself. It's much safer if I take Faith and go underground again. He'll realize we aren't here pretty fast, I'm sure, and then everyone in Zephyr will be out of danger."

"Let me decide what's best for me." His heart beat *thump-THUMP*, *thump-THUMP* in his chest, accelerating each moment that ticked by, wondering whether Dinah would allow him to go with her.

"I want you to come with us. But the last time I was running from Mickey, it was just me—I was still pregnant with Faith, so that made it easier. It was one person, not two or even three. The more of us there are, the more likely someone will spot us."

"The more of us there are, the better we can protect ourselves," Faith chimed in. "You didn't raise me to be a delicate flower who needed a man to take care of her."

"No." Dinah stepped out of Arlan's reach and stomped her foot like a petulant child. "You do not understand. Hell, the FBI doesn't understand how dangerous and deranged Mickey is." She looked at Faith. "He'd rather see us dead than living our lives without him. That's how much of a narcissist he is. And he believes that we're better off hiding from the law with him." Then she turned to Arlan. "He'd torture you if he got his hands on you. One of his men complimented me and he called him into his office and shot him in the head. I can't have your death on my conscience. I'd never survive it."

"What about going to the FBI with this information?" Arlan asked. "Maybe they can...do something? Work out a plan to catch the bastard so you're safe?"

"I—" Dinah paused and took a shuddering breath. "I think he's infiltrated the FBI."

"This is a long shot, but what if we talk to the town council? They're in your shit already—what if they have a connection to the feds and can guarantee our safety if we cooperate to catch Malone?" Faith pulled out a kitchen chair and melted into it, more tired-looking than Arlan had ever seen her.

"You know," Dinah said as she pivoted and started pacing around the kitchen, "that might be a good idea—but we'll still have to go into hiding to control the situation." She glanced at Arlan. "We still need you to take Mac until we know it's safe for us to come back home."

"I'll take a temporary separation over a permanent one any day," he said.

Faith nodded. "What about reaching out to Papa Nate and Granny Olivia? Papa's like the highest rank on the council."

"Good idea. Can you call Granny Olivia and see if we can come over to visit with her and Grandpa Nate? Do *not* give her any details—"

"I know, I know. The more she knows, the more dangerous it is for her." Faith bobbed her head.

The weight on Arlan's chest lifted. He took a deep breath for the first time since school ended and he realized Dinah wasn't in her classroom and that Faith rescheduled the debrief. "This will work. And I realize it's not ideal for you two to go into hiding for a bit, but you're right. It's for the best. I'll take Mac with me."

"And I'll call Janae and let her know I need a few days off. But Arlan? Take my work keys. Just in case we can't come back." Her lower lip quivered.

"That's not going to happen." He grasped her shoulders. "Look at me." He reached for Faith. "Get over here, you."

He pulled them into a hug. "This is going to work. It has to—because I'm not ready to give up. I'll go down fighting if necessary. You both are so important to me."

We're going to be together—one way or another.

chapter nine

You should come to me, Regina. With our daughter. It'll be so much easier if you do. And it'll make us all happy.

You dumb bitch. Answer me. I know you're getting these.

I see how this is going to go down. I didn't want it to come to this.

My daughter deserves to know who I am. Have you even told her? Or have you kept it a secret?

"Mom?" Faith called from the living room. "Granny said to come over about seven. She said to come alone, though—well, I can come with you, but specifically not Mr. DeSalvo, er, Arlan." She rolled her eyes and then crossed her arms in front of her.

Dinah got up from the table with her coffee and went into the living room, settling on the couch with Faith.

Arlan followed and Dinah scooted over to make room for him.

"It's five now. How 'bout I make something for dinner—"

"Ugh. I cannot think about food right now," Faith said.

"I can toss together something from whatever's in the fridge. You two chill." Arlan kissed Dinah on the cheek and went back into the kitchen.

"What's the plan?" Faith asked, then swiped Dinah's phone. "I need to know what the texts say."

Dinah rested her hand on top of Faith's. "Honey, you don't. He's unhinged and the messages are getting worse since I haven't answered. They'll escalate and get graphic." Dinah slipped her device out of Faith's hands and stuck it in her pocket.

"The Armbrusters are probably going to want to see those, you know."

Dinah nodded. "Yup. But only if they have a secure contact that can protect us." She sipped her coffee. "No one needs to see his poison unless they can help us stay safe and keep our friends safe—which means they'll need to have some pretty fancy connections."

"You've really thought about this."

"I've been running from him since I learned I was pregnant with you." Dinah slipped her arm around Faith's shoulders. "The first time I left, he found me and what he threatened?" Dinah shuddered. "I can't even repeat it."

The sound of birds outside near the bird feeder filled the silence in the room. Occasional rattles and clanks from Arlan's cooking adventure came from the kitchen.

"When I escaped the next time, I had help from the FBI. They put me in witness protection after I divulged everything I knew about Mickey's business dealings. But he found me again, and I was lucky he sent one of his men to get me so the feds couldn't catch him. Gunnar Meyer brought a bunch of cash with him—he collected from some of Mickey's men on the down-low—and told me not to trust the FBI and witness protection because Mickey had a mole. Which is how he's evaded capture."

"And probably how he found you," Faith added.

Arlan appeared in the archway to the kitchen. "I wonder what's changed. What's he into now that allowed him to find you after all these years?"

"So, is my real name Faith? And what's yours?"

"Your birth certificate says your name is Faith Leigh James. Mine says Regina Ellis Fontaine."

Arlan went back into the kitchen and reappeared holding a mug. He leaned against the doorframe. "I like 'Dinah' better." He smiled, and the intensity drew her in so much she almost forgot about Mickey.

Dinah's gaze shifted from Faith to Arlan and back. "I have new birth certificates and passports for us, Faith. We can disappear and get some more time before we have to change identities again—but we'll have to keep doing this as long as Mickey draws breath and walks free."

"Which is why it's important to talk to Granny Olivia and Papa Nate. They always seem to 'know a guy.'"

"How do we know the Armbrusters aren't responsible for Mickey's recent contact?" Arlan asked.

"That's a great point, but you know how intense your interview was before you were even considered for the teaching position, right?" Dinah said.

"True. And they don't like newcomers here, so why would they invite a ne'er-do-well like Mickey into town by sharing information?" Arlan added.

"Also, I stayed with Granny Olivia when I was little

while Mom worked. The Armbruster family has practically adopted us," Faith mentioned.

Arlan nodded. "Makes sense that you'd trust them."

"Dinner smells good. How long?" Dinah asked.

Arlan glanced behind him, toward the stove. "According to the timer, the pasta will be done in three minutes, so we could probably start moseying."

Dinah crossed the room and stepped into his embrace.

Faith joined them. "I thought it'd be weird having you here a lot, but it's not—I'm glad you're here. Thank you."

They stood, connected without words, until the timer with its shrill *beep-beep-beep* repeating pattern sounded, causing the trio to jump.

"Looks like dinner is served." Arlan extricated himself from the tangle and kissed Dinah's forehead before he silenced the timer and turned off the burner and then drained the pasta into a waiting colander.

Faith set the table in silence and Dinah gravitated toward the stove, lifting the lid on the medium-sized pot and inhaling. "Mmm. This Alfredo smells amazing. What's this?" She reached for the lid on a skillet sitting on the back burner.

"Sautéed mushrooms in a wine reduction. I thought about adding some of the cubed chicken in there but decided to go with just the 'shrooms."

Dinah nodded. "Good idea. We love mushrooms," she picked one out of the pan, "and these are delicious! Faith, come try this. I want the recipe."

Arlan chuckled. "There isn't one—I used what was around and it turned out. I have no idea how much I put in of anything and have likely already forgotten what I added."

"Perfect amount of garlic," Faith said.

Dinah nodded. "I can't wait to have them with the Alfredo."

"Get out of my way so I can get this pasta ready, then!" Arlan laughed.

And while the meal was delicious—Arlan had wilted some spinach in the noodles before serving—Faith pushed food around her plate, barely eating.

Dinah's small portion was more than she could handle, what with the riot of bees buzzing in her belly.

Arlan, who usually had a healthy appetite, played with his food, creating patterns with the fettuccine.

"Enough, already," Dinah said. She shoved back from the table and started to pace. "I know this seems pretty bleak, but neither of you have done this before. I know what I'm doing, and I think the Armbrusters can help."

"Okay, but what does it mean for all the friends I've made?" Faith asked. "And what about you and Arlan? How will that work?"

Dinah stopped in her tracks. "My goal is to make sure Mickey isn't able to affect our lives anymore." She pinned Arlan with an intense gaze. "And while we might have to hide out for a bit, I know that we'll get our chance to see if what we have can stand the test of time."

"I've been waiting for you for all my life, Dinah. I can wait a little longer."

Dinah moved around the kitchen again, pausing behind Arlan and placing a kiss on his cheek. "That's exactly how I feel, too."

"Good. Because I'm staying here tonight if you are."

Faith grinned like the Cheshire Cat. "Ooh. Mom's

having a sleepover with Arlan." Mischief danced in her eyes.

"Faith. That's enough." Dinah sighed. "I think we should have our things in the car, ready to leave at a moment's notice."

Arlan nodded. "Make sure you get a different vehicle if the Armbrusters send you away. Never know—he might have a device on your SUV to track it."

"I'm confident the Armbrusters can help." Dinah looked from Faith to Arlan and back.

And if they can't? I can do this again—I've already done it once.

"SO, tell me about this girl you're interested in." Jed DeSalvo wasn't one to mince words.

While he loved his dad, Arlan couldn't handle a long discussion about Dinah with things so up in the air. *Will she be here in the morning?* "It's new, Dad. I don't want to jinx anything."

"Gimme something, son. C'mon." The patriarch needled—which usually would make Arlan give in.

Not this time. "Seriously? I said I didn't want to talk about my new relationship—we're testing the waters, and the town council isn't too keen on the idea of two teachers being involved. Until I know more, please, let it go."

"That sounds like a lot to deal with. I'm sorry I pressured you—I thought you were downplaying things until you were sure. I can tell by the tone of your voice and your expression this is bothering you. Anything I can do?"

A torrent of feelings saturated his skin, and he wished he could manipulate the computer and lose the connection—but not hurt the device. After all, they weren't cheap to fix or replace.

"No, but thanks for caring. We've got some things to work out and I think the next day or two will be telling."

His father had known the love of his life would leave Earth and he'd had time to come to terms with it.

Arlan didn't have that kind of time—and didn't know whether any separation would be short-term or permanent.

"It's hard because I think she's The One, but I don't want to lose my job because of some antiquated morals clause."

"Arlan Jacob DeSalvo. What have you done?"

"Oh—nothing. I mean, she was at my house on Sunday afternoon for a few hours and the busybodies contacted the school administrator by the next morning."

"That isn't immoral. Why are people complaining?"

"There's a vague morals clause in my contract. Basically, if they deem my behavior immoral, they can terminate my employment—but they will need to provide a severance package."

"Is your paramour concerned about it?"

Arlan shook his head. "Not in the slightest. As a matter of fact, she's also not from Zephyr and thinks the morals clause was added after she joined the staff."

"Oh? How long ago was that?" Jed DeSalvo, prosecuting attorney for the City of Grand Rapids, had put Arlan on the stand once again.

"Dad. Stop it. I'm not going to let you cross-examine me."

"Excuse me? I was not—"

"You were, and you know it." Arlan grinned for a moment before the solemnity of the situation resurfaced. "This is really hard."

"Understood, son. Sorry about that."

"When are you going back to work?" Arlan asked.

"The attorney general called, asking the same question today. I told them I was ready, but the mayor insisted I take two more weeks. I think his exact words were, 'Losing someone you were so close to? That's got to be a lot to handle. I want you to know we care about you and have a therapist for you to chat with whenever you want to come back.' Isn't that some crock of horseshit? He went on to imply that I needed a psych clearance to return to work. Make sure I'd 'grieved enough' or some other bullshit story."

"I could see that if Mom had died in a crime. Like something you regularly prosecuted. But she died from cancer—fuck cancer, by the way—and you don't prosecute cells." Each conversation they had—from the time his mom, Angela, received the uterine cancer diagnosis, contained a "fuck cancer" statement. It's what they did and how they handled their grief.

"It's not just me thinking it's weird, then." The elder DeSalvo nodded. "Thanks, Arlie."

Arlan shrugged and heat raced up his chest and neck. Gratitude was one thing he'd never learned to accept. Death? It's part of life. Taxes? Another of life's guarantees. But this? "Does that go too far, legally? You're the hot-shot lawyer."

"It's a gray area. Regulating lawyers is something that isn't well defined. Some firms are stricter than others, and because I work for the city, I report to every person living in Grand Rapids."

"I know your job is much more stressful than it was when you were an assistant prosecutor. How can I help?" Arlan asked.

"You're still in the beginning stages of your new position—you focus on that. Sometimes I just need to vent, that's all."

Arlan nodded. "I'll start asking whether you want a response or whether it's rhetorical."

"Thanks, son. Now, have you solved any fun math problems lately?"

"Nah. But we will in a few weeks. I haven't told you—but I'll be getting certified to teach AP calculus courses over the summer."

"That's pretty damn cool, if you ask me."

Arlan nodded. "And I think I've managed to establish a classroom routine even though we haven't been in school a month yet."

"And how did the play go? Weren't they doing *A Midsummer Night's Dream*?"

"Yes—and it was amazing. They only do a one-weekend run and then start the next performance with tryouts after a week break. We'll have those on Monday, Tuesday, and Wednesday next week."

"What are you doing?"

"A modern-day *Funny Girl*—several young women are perfect for the role of Fanny Bryce. And we have some talented screenwriters who worked over the summer to adapt the content to lean more toward the twenty-first century."

"Let me know when to come see it. Sounds interesting."

The silence between them spoke volumes.

"Listen, Dad. There's more to the stuff going on here that I can't talk about, and I'm preoccupied with it. Can I call you midweek?"

"Was wondering when you'd come clean. Can't imagine what a teacher would have to keep from their lawyer father... Let me know if there's anything I can do to help, son. You know I'll move mountains for you."

Arlan glanced away from the screen, composing himself, before bringing his attention back to his father's face. "I know, Dad. That's why it's so hard to be all casual with you right now. I suspect you *could* help, but I can't talk about it yet."

"I get it, Arlie. Let me know when you can, and we'll get it straightened out."

"The problem is, it's not my story to tell."

"Understood. If that lady-friend of yours needs help, I'm here for it."

Arlan smiled. "I love you, Dad. Talk later." He ended the video call.

He checked the time. *Three hours since Dinah was scheduled to meet the Armbrusters. What the fuck is going on?*

He opened his text thread with her. Nothing new. Nothing from Faith, either.

Vibrating with energy, he started a load of laundry, the dishwasher, and got a bucket ready to mop the floor.

He must've been moving too fast when the mop tipped over the bucket, sending water cascading across the kitchen.

"Oh, shit!" He held his hands in front of him, parallel to the floor. The spread of the sudsy liquid stopped.

What the hell?

And then, the water drew up toward his palms, collecting in his skin—his body absorbing the moisture.

When the floor was dry, Arlan shook his head. "I must be overtired. That…couldn't have actually happened."

A low chuckle sounded behind him. "It's about time you found your powers, Arlan DeSalvo."

Arlan whipped around to face Nate Armbruster. "Aren't you supposed to be with Dinah?"

"She's fine." Nate waved off Arlan's concern. "What's important here is that you finally can explore what you can do to keep Dinah and Faith safe without the rest of the town complaining a single bit."

Puzzled, Arlan replied. "With all due respect, sir, what the hell are you talking about?"

Nate shook his head. "It's obvious. You're a witch and have water powers."

chapter ten

"Really, Dinah, I'm not sure what you want us to do here," Olivia Armbruster said, brushing away the white shock of hair that had fallen into her eyes.

"I think it's dangerous to tell you too much. What else could I tell you to persuade you to talk with the council to see if there's any way we can set up extra eyes on my house and the school in case one of my ex's associates shows up? What kind of information do you need? I've already told you he's a very bad man and has connections inside witness protection and the FBI." Dinah sighed, pacing the length of the senior Armbrusters' living room.

Olivia pursed her lips, pinning Dinah with a stare that looked deep into her soul—searching for the truth and eager to reveal any lies.

Good thing I know better than to concoct partial truths— it's so hard to keep them straight. Dinah stopped in front of Olivia—a coffee table between them. She gazed into ice-blue eyes that had seen so much.

And had been behind goings on in Zephyr in recent years.

"Start at the beginning. This man is Faith's father—you must've felt something for him at some point."

"Granny, with all due respect, I don't really think this has anything to do with the help we need right now. If my mom is scared, I trust her to know what my sperm donor is capable of."

Olivia arched an eyebrow and considered Faith for a few beats. "That might be true, but the council has the safety of the entire town to consider."

Faith stood and moved from her place on the couch to stand next to Dinah. She took a deep breath and opened her mouth.

Dinah elbowed her gently before she whispered, "I did care about him. Until I knew what he was capable of. The things he'd done." She pressed her lips together and took a deep breath. "He's responsible for the deaths of at least a half-dozen people that I'm aware of." She glanced at Faith and grabbed her hand, lacing their fingers. "And he did a bunch of illegal things—running drugs, extortion, to name a couple. There's some sketchy stuff he's been involved in, and I'm not sure whether they were his projects, or he was performing duties for others."

"That's more like it. And what prompted you to leave him?"

"Faith—at the time, she wasn't born, as you know." She whispered to her daughter, "Can you go sit in the kitchen for a few minutes? With your headphones set so you can't hear what I'm saying?"

The teen opened her mouth and then closed it, nodding.

"I made oatmeal-raisin cookies—they're in the jar.

Help yourself to a couple. Milk's in the fridge if you need it," Olivia said, her expression soft.

After Faith left the two women, Olivia said—very matter-of-factly, "That girl is nearly a legal adult. What might you have to say that you can't say in front of her?"

"Her father threatened to kill us both—he always maintained that if he couldn't have us, no one would. And I'm so frightened he might follow through this time. Look at these texts." She opened the messages and handed the device to Olivia.

The older woman's expression tightened, and she gasped. "Oh, child. You let me make a few calls. I'll see if we can get you some help." She handed the cell back to Dinah. "We do have one more matter to discuss. Arlan DeSalvo."

Dinah rolled her eyes.

"Don't you get an attitude, missy."

Her serious countenance raised red flags for Dinah. "Sorry, Olivia. I think it's ridiculous that some people think it's any of their business that Arlan and I might be involved —and that there's a morals clause in his contract." She paced away from the Armbruster matriarch. On her return, she said, "What is it that the council has a problem with?"

"Child, you sit down before you wear a groove in my maple floor." Olivia pointed to the wing-back chair to her left and waited for Dinah to settle.

"What's so special about Arlan?"

Dinah's brows knit and she considered her response before uttering a word—Olivia waited.

"He's kind. I don't want to be disrespectful—the people of Zephyr have always been nice, but I've never felt like I truly belong here. With Arlan, I feel like I might have a chance to create a place where we both belong."

"What do you mean by that?"

Dinah sighed. "The town council has a lot of power. I've never heard of a local government taking so much interest in the hiring practices of a school district. While my interview process was pretty rigorous, from what Arlan says, it's more intense now."

"It's a different time, politically. We have to be more cautious about who we allow around our children and who we let live in our town."

"Oh, I understand that. And I appreciate the fact that we're allowed to teach actual history instead of some of the revisionist...."

"Revisionist bullshit?" Olivia supplied.

Dinah chuckled. "Exactly. And everyone in town believes in science, vaccines, and the greater good."

"We've worked quite hard to keep it that way. And we don't want that to change. Newcomers need to have the same beliefs we've been promoting for over two centuries. That everyone belongs, and that Zephyr is a place where all can feel safe being their authentic selves." Olivia pinned her with an icy stare. "You see what a mess the rest of the country is in. We don't want any of that here."

"I do understand—wholeheartedly. I do, however, want to know what the problem is with Arlan and me being romantically involved."

"You don't know everything about Arlan DeSalvo. He doesn't even know everything about himself. I can't say any more right now. Soon, though, Arlan will be able to fill you in—once he understands it himself, of course."

"Forgive my language, but that's cryptic as fuck and I

don't appreciate the insinuation that Arlan and I haven't considered every angle of our relationship. We have, and can assure you—"

"That's enough, Dinah. I'm not going to argue with you. Just know that we believe you and Arlan *can* be together—there're a few details to work through first. And before you get your panties in a twist, this kibosh is coming from Nate and me—not the rest of the council."

Air *whoosh*ed out of her lungs, and she slumped back in her chair before recovering. "I— I don't know what to say. I thought we had a good relationship. You're like Faith's grandmother. Hannah is the sister I always wanted —and I've felt so blessed to have your family open your arms to us. This feels like... like a betrayal. Why couldn't you come to me about this?"

Olivia placed her hand on Dinah's thigh. "It's not my story to tell—and Arlan, the poor thing—has some hard truths to come to terms with in the next little bit. He'll talk to you when he's ready. And when he does? Everything will make sense. Well, as long as he does decide to confide in you, which I very much suspect he will."

"He will, Nana. Arlan loves my mom, and she loves him—even though they're too chicken to actually say it." Faith smiled. "Oh, the cookies are really good. Did you do something different?"

"Can't pull one over on you, can I?" Olivia chuckled. "I used applesauce instead of butter. Lowers the fat."

Olivia glanced around the room and paused, inhaling and exhaling a few times.

"I need you two to wait for a few minutes while I make a couple of calls. But in the meantime? I want you to turn off those cell phones. I don't know if you're being tracked or not, and I'd appreciate it if we had some lead time to get you some protection."

"They're in airplane mode. We thought about that already. But Arlan's going to be worried if I don't contact him soon."

Olivia waved her off. "Nate's with him."

"Why's Papa over at Arlan's?"

Olivia considered her response, a smirk slipping across her face. "You sure do ask a lot of questions and have lots of opinions, young lady."

Faith grinned. "I think I got half of 'em from you, so you should be super proud of me."

All three women laughed.

"Go help yourself if you're hungry. There're leftovers out there."

Dinah shook her head. "Oh, we ate earlier and we're planning dessert once we get home. We've got some ice cream we want to eat in case we need to leave town."

Olivia smirked. "You're not going anywhere. Just wait."

NATE SNAPPED his fingers and fire danced at the end of each digit. "You have to learn how to control it, son."

Arlan's head whipped up, his attention pinning Nate Armbruster with an icy glare. "Please don't call me 'son.' That's reserved for my dad."

Holding his hands up in front of him, Nate said, "Sorry. No offense. Just a term of endearment."

"So, tell me again how I came to be a witch and have water powers. My brain isn't comprehending."

"You're adopted, right?" Nate asked.

Arlan's head bobbed up and down.

"At least one of your biological parents is a witch, then. I suspect only one parent is, though. Normally, if you get the gene from both parents, you'd likely have had this day come by the time you were a teenager, if not before."

"Why does it take longer if there's only a single set of witch DNA?"

"Because you weren't around people with powers, they sat dormant until you reached Zephyr. There's quite a group of us here—and before you ask, I won't identify any of the other families. All of us Armbrusters are witches—that includes Hannah and Kennedy."

"So, is it a rule that I have to marry a witch or something?" Arlan gasped. "Oh, this is what this bullshit from the council is about—the whole 'morals clause' in my contract. You're worried that if Dinah and I get together that we'll have a kid that's not a pureblooded witch."

"You couldn't be further from the truth. We hope you'll confide in Dinah after you understand what's going on. It's going to take a while to get your powers under control, so you know how to use them. And if you truly want Dinah and Faith in your life after you know the consequences of telling them, then we welcome it. It's been a pain in the ass to keep it from her all these years—not to mention the fact that Olivia has to actually wash dishes instead of doing them with magic when Dinah and Faith are around, and we can't occupy them in another room." Nate chuckled. "She bitches up a storm and has threatened to tell them at least three or four times a year since Faith was born."

"So why haven't you?" Arlan asked.

Nate shrugged. "It didn't feel right. And now we know why—it's always been your job to tell Dinah about us."

Arlan nodded. "Okay, I see, sort of. What I don't get is why you didn't come out and tell me. Maybe pull me aside once I hit town and mention it?"

Sighing, Nate shook his head. "Would you have believed me?"

"I suppose not."

"We've been keeping an eye on you—your magic has been getting stronger. Kennedy has been instrumental in making sure we approached you at the right time. She saw you stir your coffee the other day—by circling your finger over the cup. We didn't know whether you had air or water powers, though."

"It's obvious I am going to need a tutor of some sort—to figure out how to not use my magic impetuously."

"That's definitely going to be the biggest challenge. We thought Hannah had water powers, but it turns out she's special and has a talent for healing. Convenient, she's a nurse, right?" Nate chuckled again.

"So, is there anyone in town who has water powers?"

"Don't get your knickers in a twist. I'll find you someone to help you learn about your powers, who is also a water witch. I'll have them email or text in a few days. In the meantime, there are some rules."

"Of course there are rules." Arlan rolled his eyes.

"You're sassy like Dinah. She's going to have her hands full if you and Faith ever decide to gang up on her."

He shook his head. "Nate, I'll never side with Faith against her mom. That's not how I roll."

"Good to hear. Dinah is like a second daughter to me,

and Faith is as much my grandchild as Kennedy—except for the whole manipulating fire thing."

Nate's phone *pinged*, and he checked it. "I'm supposed to tell you everything is okay with Dinah and Faith—they're at my place with Olivia. Livvie is making some calls to see if we can get Dinah in touch with our contact in the FBI."

"Wait. There's a witch in the FBI?"

Nate nodded. "And some shifters and vampires. A couple fae, last I heard."

Slowly blinking, Arlan said, "Shifters...as in werewolves?"

Sliding one shoulder up to nearly his ear, Nate said, "They hate it when you use that term. They're wolf shifters. You wouldn't say 'werepossum,' would you? Of course not." He rolled his eyes.

Arlan laugh-snorted. "A werechipmunk."

"Now you're just mocking them."

"I suppose I can suspend disbelief. After all, when I got up this morning, I never thought I was a water witch or that I could use my hands to clean up spilled mop water."

"That's the spirit. Now, the shifters aren't affected by the moon's phases. However, they do tend to gather under the full moon because they can do things at night with the light of the moon and not worry about the humans in town finding out."

"I'll be frank—I wasn't going to pigeon-hole them into stereotypes."

"Good. Then you won't be surprised when I tell you that vampires don't sparkle, aren't burned by the sun, and eat more than blood. The garlic thing has a grain of truth—when a vampire consumes garlic, they have bad breath for a *long* time. Even if they brush their teeth, gargle with mouthwash, use a salt rinse,and then baking soda to brush their teeth—the halitosis is barely manageable."

"I'm going to guess they don't have the stereotypical weaknesses, too, then."

"Correct," Nate murmured. "You'll likely never have to hurt these creatures—and if you do have occasion to do so, you'll want to use your magic. It'll catch them off guard. We're all on the same side—we want a safe place to raise our families and for the next generation to settle into life in Zephyr."

"So, if you have generations of people here, why do you need to hire a math teacher from outside Zephyr?"

Nate leaned forward, bracing his palms on his knees. "Getting the best education possible is what's most important. Do we understand one another? You were hired on your merits as an educator. I don't want you thinking that we gave you the position because you're a witch—and that this way we can keep tabs on you."

"My brain is overloaded. So, let's say I do believe you. What's the next step?"

"Easy. Tell Dinah you're a witch and that there are others in town like you. Don't mention the other beings. It's their job to select when the best time is to reveal themselves."

Arlan nodded. "Makes sense."

"Great. Now, I think it's past time that we get to my house. If our contacts come through, it'll be better that we're all together to hear the next steps."

"What are the chances that Dinah and Faith will have to leave town?"

Nate peered at him. "Well, now. That's up to you. How fast can you learn to control those powers of yours?"

"Pretty damn fast if it means Dinah can stay."

"We'll send an unmarked officer to watch the house until you have a way to summon your powers when you need them. This is a short-term solution, though. So, I'll need you to focus on learning your defensive spells."

"Consider them perfected, Nate." Arlan reached out and the men shook hands.

"I don't doubt that you'll do everything in your power to stay with our Dinah."

"It's not just Dinah—I think Faith is amazing and have this urge to be a father figure for her. At least show her how a lady should be treated."

"You've been setting a fine example, from what we know. As a matter of fact, Olivia told Hannah and Kennedy that you're a lot like a younger version of me. Livvie is my world, as are my kids and grandkids."

"I feel the same way about Dinah and Faith."

"Well, you better not break her heart—"

"Nate, you don't have to worry about giving me the lecture and threatening me. Janae Brown's already done that."

"Heh. Bet she was hilarious with all her blustering five-foot-nothing telling you off."

Arlan shrugged. "She sounded fierce as hell, if I'm frank, and she scared me a little."

"Well, her kind does that."

"I was going to ask what you mean by that, but I'm guessing it's not your story to tell."

"Nope. Through the council, Janae will hear about you, and then she'll probably reveal herself."

Arlan looked at his phone again. "Shit. I forgot. They're in airplane mode."

"Let's go. I can tell you're not up to receiving more information until you see Dinah with your own two eyes."

Hopefully, she'll believe me when I tell her later—maybe I should show her instead.

"Hey, Nate? Can you help me perfect something quick? So I can show Dinah instead of telling her?"

"What more do you need? Spill a damn glass of water and soak it up. If you're sassy, you can even use your finger like a squirt gun."

Arlan retrieved a glass of water and set it on the table.

Nate's gaze locked with his.

Reaching out a big hand, Nate tipped over the water. He smirked.

Arlan twirled his index finger, pointing at the spilled liquid.

It drew up into a miniature cyclone and danced over the tabletop.

Sliding his hand underneath, Arlan lifted the tiny twister, cupping it in his palm. Then he covered it with his other hand. Pressing them together, he expected water to gush out.

When it didn't, Arlan gasped. His palms were dry, as was the table. "Well, shit. This is going to be pretty fun."

chapter eleven

"So. Let me get this straight. You're a witch and so are the Armbrusters. And there are more in Zephyr." Dinah smiled.

Arlan nodded. "I just found out a couple hours ago, so I thought I'd share the 'What the fuck-ness' with you."

She rolled her eyes and shifted her attention to the living room, where Nate and Olivia spoke in quiet tones with Faith.

Olivia said, "We can keep you safe, but you need to follow everything we say. Do you think you can do that?"

Faith nodded.

Nate said something she couldn't quite hear.

"I don't have a problem not having a phone. If I need to connect with anyone, there are other online services, and I can use a different device on Wi-Fi."

"You kids..." Olivia said, shaking her head.

"We plan a lot of stuff like this, Granny. I'll tell everyone I dropped my phone, and it broke—and we ordered another one. This type of thing happens all the time."

Dinah re-focused on Arlan. "That's...a lot to take in—on top of my own fuckery."

Grasping her hand, Arlan said, "You deal with mine; I'll deal with yours. The only reason there's been a problem with the council is because I didn't know I had powers, and you needed to go into this relationship knowing what all it entails."

"And that would be...?"

"Well, from what Nate said, now that you're in the know, we need you to promise you won't ever reveal the truth about Zephyr to anyone."

Dinah nodded. "That's easy. All my friends are here, and I don't have family."

"You do, just not blood relatives. Nate and Olivia think of you as their bonus daughter, and it's killed them to not tell you all these years."

"I always sensed there was something up and that everyone wasn't being straight with me." She sighed. "I guess that explains why Olivia insists on cleaning up after meals and why the family always goes for a walk or into the game room after dinner while she does it. She's using magic and didn't want me to find out!" Dinah laughed. "I'm a little jealous."

"Well, if that's something I can learn, there's no need for you to be jealous because I'll handle dishes as long as you continue to cook. Your food is amazing." Arlan picked up her hand and kissed her knuckles. "So, you're totally on board?"

Dinah nodded.

"Then I guess it's time for us to hear all about this FBI agent and what his directions are for us."

She stood, pressing her hands against the table. Bone-deep weariness saturated her body.

Arlan rose and reached out to her. "Whatever the message is, we'll come up with a plan."

Dinah nodded again. "We will. It'll be fine."

"It'll be better than fine—we have each other and together, along with Faith and our Zephyr family, we'll manage and come out the other side ready to take on the world and get on with the rest of our lives."

"What about your dad?" Dinah asked.

"I've thought about this. I don't think he needs to know. He's quite concrete and I think the lawyer in him will rebel and need to know the 'whys' instead of taking the leap of faith." He paused and looked away for a moment before returning his attention to Dinah. "But if he decides to move here after retirement—he's mentioned it a couple times—we'll have to revisit the topic."

"That sounds reasonable. Now. To tell Faith."

"That's your call. If you think it's too much for her to handle right now—with the stuff going on with Mickey—we can wait. But I do think she needs to know. It'll explain a helluva lot that goes on in Zephyr."

Dinah nodded again. "Definitely. Which is why I think it's important to tell her now. So she understands there'll be things at play we may *not* understand at this time, but will continue to learn more about them as time passes."

"That's a great way to look at it. Let's go tell her. Together."

Dinah stepped into Arlan's arms, resting her head on his chest, and listened to the solid beat of his heart. *Thump-THUMP, thump-THUMP, thump-THUMP.*

He rested his cheek on the top of her head, breathing deeply. "I could do this for the rest of my life."

"I hope you want to—since I know all about your witchy-woo-woo now, we're sort of stuck with each other."

"There's no one else I'd rather be stuck with." Arlan put space between them and then, with his index finger, coaxed Dinah's chin upward and brushed his lips against hers.

Rising up on her toes, Dinah deepened the kiss, sweeping her tongue against his bottom lip before sighing. "We'll have to continue this later. When we don't have an audience." Her gaze refocused on the occupants of the living room.

Faith smiled. "Dinah and Arlan, sitting in a tree. K-I-S-S-I-N-G." She sang.

"You better watch it, young lady. The day you decide to bring a boy home? Remember, turnabout is fair play," Dinah said.

They all laughed and settled in the comfortable living room space.

"So, Faith," Dinah started.

"Let me guess. It's okay for you and Arlan to be together now?"

Arlan nodded. "That's part of it."

"You're telling her now?" Olivia asked.

"We are. It's important she understands everything that might happen," Dinah said.

"Well then," Nate said, "let's start with some history. This'll be a great lesson for the three of you."

Dinah clapped her hands: *tap-tap-tap*. "Oh, goody!"

"I'll not go all the way back to the early 1700s—that's a story for another day," Nate started.

"Zephyr was a mining town, and after the collapse of the mine, things were pretty quiet for a while. But then, it became a hotbed for paranormal beings. We think it's because of the mine, but no one can be sure," Olivia said.

"So, our ancestors came to Zephyr because they heard about the community where paranormal beings could live without hiding who they were. A town council consisting of two witches, two vampires, two shifters, and two fae was developed to legislate and create a strict set of rules so we could all live together in harmony. Those rules are still in place today, mostly," Nate added.

Faith's eyes were wide. "What do you mean, paranormal beings? Are you serious? What kind of beings are in Zephyr?" She glanced toward Dinah, who nodded. "And how long have you known about this?"

"Um, about ten minutes?" Dinah said.

"Oh. Okay. I was about to get a little upset that you've been keeping something this cool from me." She grinned. "So, tell me. What are you?" She looked at Olivia and Nate.

Olivia pressed her lips together and dimples formed as she held back a laugh.

"No questions?" Nate asked. "We should have told *you* first. Arlan was full of enough of them."

Arlan chuckled. "Hey, science hasn't proven that y'all exist yet."

"Oh, but it has. We've managed to keep it quiet and out of the journals and news," Olivia said.

"Really? And how—" Arlan started.

"DNA. Genetic material—something all science-y that I don't really get but makes sense according to the experts. I can send you the research if you want to take a look. It proves there is one DNA marker for witches, shifters, and fae—we're born. Vampires have a genetic mutation caused by a virus, so they acquire vampirism," Nate said.

"Eventually, I'll want to learn more. For now? It's better that I focus on controlling my powers before I dig into the research."

"Your. Powers?" Faith echoed; her expression incredulous.

"Oh, yes," Dinah said. "Arlan's a witch and can manipulate water. He just found out today."

"I— I am without words," the teen said as she looked from one adult to the next.

"Dinah? Faith? Any questions?" Olivia asked.

Dinah glanced at Faith, who shook her head. "We trust you—we don't need to know the 'how' right now. Maybe later—once we're safe from Mickey."

Nate cleared his throat. "If there aren't other questions about the existence of paranormal beings, let's talk about Mickey Malone and the huge mistake he made when he contacted you again."

"FIRST, Dinah, we wish you would've confided in us a lot sooner. We could've had this taken care of a long time ago," Olivia said.

"It's not like I knew you had magical powers or anything." Dinah rolled her eyes. "If you *had* told me, I would've come clean because I'd've figured you had a trick or two up your sleeves that might help keep us safe."

"Honestly, Mom. Would you have, though? With how unhinged you say the sperm donor is—"

Olivia interrupted. "Oh, he is Faith. I'm glad your mom has kept his messages from you. He's…sick."

"Regardless, I don't think Mom would've told you because she'd've wanted to protect you, even though you have magic on your side."

Dinah bobbed her head from side to side, considering Faith's proclamation. "There's likely a little truth to that."

"Anyway," Nate jumped in, "since we started a community here in Zephyr, paranormal beings have become united around the world. There are a few other communities like ours, but not many."

Olivia added, "This means we have a broader network of contacts than we'd have if we were isolated covens of witches connected by some international governing board —which is how things were back in the early days of Zephyr. It wasn't until the last thirty years that this sort of coexisting between paranormals has happened around the world."

"We have people in all levels of state and federal government. In every important office. Like the FBI." Nate looked from Dinah to Faith, his gaze finally landing on Arlan. "This means we've reached out to one of our FBI contacts—who is a shifter—and explained your situation."

Olivia jumped in. "I've got this—I actually spoke to the agent." She set her hand on Nate's arm.

He slid his arm back to lace their fingers.

"To make a long story short, you're staying in town. We're getting the senior members of our coven together in a few hours to start working on some spells to protect you. By morning, we should have those in place."

"Are these something I can learn?" Arlan asked.

"Well, maybe you can re-set them—but we want a

group of three of our most powerful witches to cast them initially. That'll be Olivia and two other witches—they have the strongest magic when it comes to household and family," Nate said.

"But it'll be important for you to learn the spells, Arlan. We'll teac you so you can 'touch up' the wards—we want to keep things as normal as possible if Mickey has eyes inside Zephyr."

Dinah gasped and slid her arm through Arlan's, drawing herself into him. "Do you think there's anyone in town who could be doing that?"

"We're not sure, but if anyone can find out, it's our FBI agent contact. Especially if they're using technology to communicate with him." Nate's voice dropped into a lower register. "And if we find out that's happening, they'll rue the day they thought they could betray one of us."

"Awww. That's super sweet and all, but how are you realistically going to keep the sperm donor from abducting us or hurting someone we love?" Faith asked.

"Good question. We'll put up wards around the town that should only allow people and vehicles we've granted access to enter the town limits. You might have never noticed, but Zephyr can be a bit like a gated community. We have a guard shack on the road into town—about a mile from the turnoff from Petoskey."

"I noticed it when I moved to town. I wondered why it was there," Arlan said.

"And I've *never* noticed it," Dinah said.

"We've been masking it from the humans in town. No need to alert anyone that there's a chance we could close the community, so no one goes in or out." Nate took a sip of water from a metal cup. "And about half the town is human and has no clue Beings exist. We'd like to keep it that way." He looked from Arlan to Dinah, with his eyes coming to rest on Faith.

The teen nodded. "Oh, I get it. I don't think talking about this topic without knowing who exactly the Beings in town are is a very good idea."

Arlan snort-laughed.

Everyone chuckled.

"There's a directory. If you're interested in locating a wolf shifter, for example, you'd search in the directory by Being type. You can then arrange from youngest to oldest —and vice versa," Olivia said. "I'll be sure Arlan gets access to our password-protected server where all of these documents live and can be retrieved via a little well-worded search, eventually."

"This is all so...fantastical." Arlan slid his arm around Dinah. "But we'll manage, and I'll learn how to keep my family safe."

Dinah's head whipped to face him. Tears welled along her waterline. "Your family?"

Arlan nodded. "If you'll have me."

Faith launched over the coffee table and wrapped her arms around them. "Are you kidding? It'll be *great* to call you family!" She paused, tipped her head. "I don't think I'm cool calling you 'Dad,' though."

"Yup. That'd be weird." Arlan laughed.

Olivia shook her head. "I don't know how you aren't freaking out. I grew up with witches and had a moment when I learned there were additional paranormal Beings."

"It's okay to believe in things we don't understand." Dinah shifted to face Olivia and Nate. "Now, how 'bout a demonstration of some of these magical powers?"

"You're in luck. I haven't cleaned in a couple days." Olivia grinned, then stood.

Cleanliness and purification,
Wrought through mystical translation.
When this rhyme is spoken true,
Dust and grime, I banish you!

A small whirlwind—five or six inches tall—appeared in the living room in front of Olivia. She gave it a little tap, and it zipped around the room above all the flat surfaces. It drew dust and trash into itself and moved other items— like the television remote—to clean under them before moving on to the next spot.

As it went over the rug, it widened and nestled into the carpet a little bit, leaving vacuum tracks—just like would appear in a *regular* home while cleaning.

When the cyclone finished in the living room, it settled in front of Olivia again, shrinking to bring it down to around two inches in height, who picked it up like Arlan had the tiny twister in his kitchen. She cupped her hands, shrinking the cleaning dervish, and collapsing it into her palms. Blowing into her hands, she spread them in front of her. No dust, no waste.

"Oh, Arlan. You *definitely* need to learn to do that," Dinah whispered, her voice filled with awe.

Nate produced a glass of water. "Show her what you *can* do, Arlan." And then he poured the water onto the wood coffee table. It dribbled off the side, into the rug.

Faith gasped.

Arlan repeated the twirling motion with his finger and a tiny tornado formed, sucking up the water on the table before skittering over the edge to the carpet. After recalling the twister, he absorbed the water and collapsed the cyclone.

Dinah reached down and brushed her fingertips over the rug. "It's perfectly dry—like it never had water on it at all!"

"You know, this could be super helpful in cleaning the set pieces in the drama storage unit," Faith added. "It can be a real pain to get them clean—and there's always dust because it's so hard to keep things covered when we're cramming as much as we can in there."

"That sounds like a great use of my newfound talent, some day," Arlan commented. "But one thing's for certain: I'm one hundred percent sure that with the Zephyr coven's help, I can keep you safe from Mickey Malone—and hopefully ensure that he never bothers us again."

chapter twelve

Back in her own home, Dinah moved around the space she shared with Faith, ensuring that she locked all the doors and windows and closed the window treatments to keep out prying eyes.

"Still. I think we need to consider sleeping in shifts tonight. At least until the Armbrusters can get our house protected from strangers to Zephyr." Faith followed behind her, babbling—which was how Dinah knew she was scared.

"Honey, Nate and Olivia said they'd have us protected by morning. And since they'll be getting things set tonight, it means they'll be outside in a bit. Please, don't worry."

They reached the open living room with its wall of windows.

"Let's keep the lights off in here as much as possible. These aren't blackout shades, so someone outside can probably see silhouettes," Arlan said, closing the last window treatment.

"I think *Charmed* is appropriate tonight. What about you, Mom?"

Dinah chuckled. "Excellent choice. I'll get the cocoa started. Arlan? Do you want some?"

"Maybe coffee instead? I'm going to stay up for a bit and make sure the coven makes it over before I rest."

Dinah wrapped her arms around him. "You're so sweet." She drew in a deep breath, taking in the scent of sandalwood and sage she'd come to associate with Arlan DeSalvo.

He kissed the top of her head. "I don't know about that—I just want to make sure my family is safe."

There it was again.

Family.

"It's strange to hear that word in connection with anyone besides Faith and me," Dinah said. "We've been doing this for so long, it might be hard to let you in and make you part of our daily routine, but" she glanced at Faith, who nodded, "we're going to try. Make sure you ask us to explain the inside jokes and why we do what we do." She tipped her chin upward and rolled up onto her toes, brushing a chaste kiss across Arlan's lips.

"You've made me feel so welcome—I can't believe how natural it is to hang out with you both in this space."

Dinah's phone vibrated in her back pocket.

Arlan placed his hand over it, shaking his head. "If it's Olivia and Nathan, they'll reach out to me. Who else could it be? Faith is here. No one else is important enough to look at that damn thing."

"What if it's Janae? Or Mara? What if...."

"Stop catastrophizing. Is that even a word?" Faith shrugged. "Regardless, you're being a Negative Nancy and that's not like you. You've always taught me to be a 'glass half full' kind of person."

"And that's what drew me to you—the positive spin you put on everything and normalized the feelings I was having as a first-year teacher."

"Plus, you know all the students think you're the 'cool' teacher, right?" Faith added.

"I'd rather be the most respected than the coolest," Dinah murmured.

"That's the thing—you're both. Sure, some people think Mara is okay, but they know they can get away with stuff in her class. With you, everyone knows where they stand because you're consistent and fair—and you tell everyone the consequences up front." Faith glanced at Arlan. "And some are even starting to think Arlan is okay —mostly because he hangs out with you."

"Popularity by distributive property." Arlan squeezed her and released before peering into the kitchen. "One thing I am not a fan of: With all the drapes closed, I can't see what's going on in the street."

Faith gasped, then flapped her hands. "Hey! We installed a couple doorbell cameras and connected the app to Mom's iPad. That might help with street activity. I mean, it's not *perfect,* but you can see what's happening— like someone is coming up the driveway, driving past. That kind of thing."

"I forgot about that." Dinah picked up the device, sitting on the end table next to her side of the couch, and then reached for the charging cable and plugged it in. "Battery's a little low, but it'll charge faster than it'll drain while we're using it." She tapped the touch screen to launch the doorbell cam app.

A wide-angle view of the side door appeared. She

switched the camera to the front door, offering a panorama of their driveway and the street.

A dark sedan crept past.

"That wasn't at all timely." Arlan's derisive tone matched Dinah's thoughts.

"I don't think the timing could have been any more perfect," she said.

Arlan held out his hands and Dinah passed him the tablet. "You two do the normal thing. It's important in case someone is watching."

Dinah shuddered. As if on cue, her phone vibrated. "I'm going to make the cocoa and some coffee." She looked at Faith. "Go ahead and get started—I can hear from the kitchen."

Her gut roiled as her phone vibrated again and she inhaled before slowly exhaling. The sensation subsided after she repeated the breathwork twice more.

She checked the living room before pulling out her phone. Arlan and Faith stared toward the TV and the opening recap before the next episode of *Charmed*.

More texts from the unknown number. Mickey.

> Welcome home. Did you have a nice visit with the Armbrusters?

> Tell your boyfriend I'm going to kill him when I pick up my daughter tonight.

> And don't bother telling good ol' Olivia and Nate—they can't help you.

A prickling sensation spread over her body, and she dropped her phone. She pressed her lips together and focused on her breathwork again.

"You okay?" He stooped and picked up her device before placing his palm on her back and rubbing slow circles.

Dinah shook her head.

He held the phone out to her, and she unlocked it, revealing the texts.

"We have a problem. He's here—or at least has eyes here."

Arlan used his phone to take a picture of the texts from Mickey. "I'm sending these to Nate."

Dinah nodded. "I'm not using my cell for anything except keeping track of his messages. He's watching everything I do, anyway."

"What's going on?" Faith said as she entered the kitchen.

Dinah glanced at Arlan.

He nodded.

"I think we need to consider being a *lot* more cautious. He's got eyes on us somehow. He knows we just got home and knows Arlan is here."

Faith rushed into her mother's arms.

"And he's threatening Arlan."

Arlan hugged them both.

"He said he's 'picking you up tonight' in this series of messages."

Faith wiggled out of their grasp.

"The fuck he is." Her steely expression reminded Dinah of the surety and hard-headedness Mickey had shown so often—even through his delusions.

She is not her father. Faith is an amazing young woman. I've raised her to be compassionate and understanding and to be kind.

Arlan stepped back. "Agreed." He looked at his phone. "Nate said he and Olivia are on their way over. They've called for some reinforcements to keep an eye out while the Three set the wards to keep us safe. They're going to the school after—so we can keep things as normal as possible."

"We need to stay away from the windows and make sure we aren't backlit so no one can tell where we are in the house," Faith said.

Dinah shook her head. "You've been watching too many crime shows."

"Maybe, but it's true." Faith shrugged her shoulders. "I'll turn off the TV. Make sure your phones are set on dark mode if you're going to use them."

A moment later, the teen switched off the screen, engulfing the interior of the house in darkness.

"Do you think we need to cover the digital clocks and remove the nightlights?" Dinah asked.

"Might be a good idea—just to make sure. I'll get the one in the hallway and make my way back here. We can put a dishtowel over the microwave to hide the clock. Same over the stove's clock," Arlan said.

Dinah's phone vibrated again. The lock screen displayed the latest missive from her unhinged ex.

> LOL. Like sitting in the dark will prevent me from knowing where you are in the house. And dark mode isn't going to help you AT ALL.

Her eyes opened wide, and she showed the message to Arlan, who took a photo and then tapped his screen a few more times.

He showed her the message he'd sent along with the screenshot.

He can hear what we're saying.

Faith re-appeared. "What's going—"

Dinah put her hand over Faith's mouth and simultaneously pressed a vertical finger to her own lips.

Faith nodded.

Dinah showed her the text.

Faith's hands flew to her mouth for a moment before she mouthed, "Oh shit."

DINAH'S TERROR was evident in her expression. She pulled Faith to her and then tucked her into her side. Protecting her the best way she could from the unseen danger.

Arlan typed a message into his notes app: The Three will be here soon. Before they start, Nate's going to try a spell to destroy or identify where the listening devices are in the house without Mickey noticing.

Faith and Dinah nodded.

Faith gave him a thumbs up.

A floorboard in the hallway creaked.

The women's focus shifted as they peered through the kitchen's archway in the sound's direction.

Another creak. This time, closer.

Arlan grabbed a knife from the butcher block and

stepped in front of Dinah and Faith, corralling them into the corner near the refrigerator.

Dinah's palm rested in the middle of his back, somehow communicating her love and trust for Arlan. And her terror vibrated from every nerve ending.

A low, sinister laugh sounded—close to the entrance to the kitchen, but not quite there yet.

"Come out, come out—wherever you are." The hair on the back of Arlan's neck stood at attention; the singsong, malevolent tone of the speaker sent up all the warnings.

Faith gasped.

"I know you're in the kitchen, little chickens. Make this easier on yourselves and no one will get hurt. Much." He laughed again.

Dinah sighed. Her hand slid across his back as she moved to his side and then in front of him.

Arlan lowered the knife.

"Mickey. I can't believe you're doing your own dirty work, for a change."

He stepped into the kitchen and flipped on the light.

"Regina. I wish I could say you looked lovely as ever, but you've really let yourself go." He paused. "Oh, yes. You go by 'Dinah' now. How silly of me."

His attention swung over Arlan's shoulder. "And you, young lady. You're absolutely lovely. Much lovelier than the name 'Faith' implies. You should be called 'Caroline.'" He reached out his right hand; his left remained tucked behind him. "Come to Daddy, Caroline."

Weapon? Arlan focused on Mickey, imagining he could stare right through him and see what was going on behind his back.

And then, the man's skin and other soft tissues melted

away. Bones became somewhat translucent, revealing a pistol.

Arlan's instincts kicked in, and he flipped the knife in his hand so its tip pointed toward the floor, his fists ready to knock the intruder on his ass.

Nate's voice sounded in his head.

Only other witches in the vicinity can hear me, so behave appropriately.

Faith pressed her forehead into the middle of his back.

"Fuck you, Mickey. Faith isn't going anywhere." Dinah's voice was strong and commanding.

Mickey recoiled slightly, as though Dinah had slapped him. He gasped. "Such language—and in front of your daughter. Regina—er, Dinah. You should be ashamed. *Tsk, tsk, tsk.*"

We should have seen this coming. It's likely he has someone on his team that can dampen some of our powers.

"Come out from behind the geek, Caroline." Mickey brandished his weapon. "Before I make you."

Faith rested the side of her cheek against Arlan's upper arm. "I don't negotiate with terrorists. Unload the gun and set it on the table." Her voice echoed in the room. Strong. Unwavering. Like her mother's.

Mickey grinned, his expression morphing into something resembling congeniality with a dash of innocence tossed in for good measure. "Does the gun scare you? It's okay if it does. You haven't been raised around them— likely, you've been trained to fear them by your granola-crunching socialist mother. It's not your fault. So, I'll do what you ask—but know it's not my *only* weapon." His grin became wider and his top canine teeth appeared to elongate.

Fuck. Fuck. Fuck. Arlan thought.

What's going on? Concentrate on thinking through each thing we need to know, Arlan.

He took a deep breath, centering himself.

Dinah and Faith took a step backward.

Arlan widened his stance and tipped the knife horizontally with the edge facing his enemy.

Time slowed.

Mickey Malone is a fucking vampire.

chapter thirteen

Mickey ran the tip of his tongue along his top teeth, slowing as he slipped it along the edge of a fang.

"You speak like you're Faith's father, but a true parent doesn't threaten the life of his child or their other parent," Dinah said.

What. The. Fuck. Vampires, too?

Arlan stood beside her: tense, frozen, focused. Like nothing would tear them apart.

Except the very creature standing before them defied logic—*but so did witches with magical powers, this morning.*

He waved her off. "That was a lifetime ago. I don't care whether you live or die anymore. I do, however, want Caroline to live forever with me." He focused his gaze on Faith. "We can have it all, baby. We'll rule the world."

Arlan murmured, "Don't look into his eyes—he can compel you to do things."

"True, true," Mickey inhaled deeply. "Witch." It didn't sound like a compliment, the way he spat it out.

"You're still the insecure little man who emotionally

and physically abused me, Mickey. *My* daughter is strong and can resist you," Dinah said. *Mickey is nervous. He's tapping his fingertips to his palms.*

"I'm bored—and children shouldn't play with knives." Mickey focused on Arlan.

A small tremor rocked the butcher knife back and forth in rapid, tiny movements, and Arlan's shoulder visibly tightened and flexed beneath his Twisted Sister T-shirt. He took a step backward, nearly pinning Faith behind him.

The teen slid behind her mother, hands shaking.

"You won't win, Malone," Arlan said through gritted teeth.

Something drew Mickey's attention. His focus dropped, and he looked around the room. "Where are they? I can sense the other witches."

"That'll be our council and our Three. They're here to protect us from you," Arlan said.

Mickey relaxed a bit and chuckled. "We'll see about that."

"Hey, Mickey? When did you become a vampire?" Dinah asked. *If I can distract him by asking questions, he won't be able to resist.*

"Do you *really* care? I don't think the 'when' matters as much as the 'why' in my case." He crossed his arms, tipping one upward to hold his chin between his index finger and thumb. "And it's not your business—but I'll allow it because my daughter likely has the same questions." He pivoted to more fully face Faith. "Do you have the same questions, my darling girl?"

"It'd be nice to know why you chose to become this way. Might help me get to know the man you are today—and maybe I'll decide you're worth my time. But that'll be a battle you'll need to win if you expect us to have any relationship moving forward."

"Unacceptable. We'll have a relationship, regardless of your wishes. As a matter of fact, I've grown bored with this interaction. Caroline? We're leaving." He held his hand out to her again and Faith started drifting toward him.

With her feet off the ground, she slipped through the small space in the kitchen until she hovered right in front of Mickey. Her sealed lips made it impossible for her to speak.

"Ah. That's much better. Children should do as they're told and be seen—not heard."

Faith struggled against invisible bonds.

Dinah's feet stuck to their spot on the floor, her arms heavy at her sides like large weights hung from them.

"Someday you'll learn to do what I say, *Dinah James*." He said her name in a tone full of derision and malice. "And if you ever intend to see your daughter again, you'll patiently wait for my instructions. There'll be no witches—no additional Beings should learn about our little *situation*." After gripping Faith's upper arm, Mickey and Faith vanished.

Mickey's effects on Dinah dissipated.

Dinah scanned the room. "They... They disappeared. Where did they go?" Turning to Arlan, she said, "You have to help me find her. She can't be alone with that monster—he'll destroy her spirit and what makes Faith who she is." She could tell her voice rose in pitch with each moment that passed, as panic set in.

Arlan pulled her into his embrace, sliding his palms up and down her back.

"Nate knows what's happened."

Tap-tap-tap.

"That'll be him." Arlan squeezed her a little tighter and released her to cross the room and open the side door. "Nate. Thanks for being here and being in my head. This witch communication thing is pretty cool."

Nate nodded. "We use it when we need to." He shrugged. "This is a situation where anything goes now."

She recognized the set of Nate's jaw, the determination in his expression. He'd had it when he met Dinah and newborn Faith and a few other times since—usually when he was being protective. "I appreciate it," she murmured after schooling her expression into one devoid of emotion.

Meeting her gaze and holding it, he said, "Dinah, you don't have to thank us. You're family. You have been for years. It's nice to be able to use our additional skill sets openly, though." He produced a tiny hammer—like one a medical professional might use to check reflexes—and placed it in his right palm.

> *By smithy's fire and raven's call,*
> *Find those who lurk beyond our walls.*
> *Let this hammer purge their ear,*
> *And protect the ones that I hold dear.*

The hammer shimmered and levitated from Nate's palm. Surrounded by a sparkling orb, it spun in the middle of the room before darting toward the ceiling near the sink. There, it tapped against the top face of the cabinet and an array of sparks fizzled around it, ash landing on the countertop.

"It'll clear each room, one by one, before moving to the next. If there are only sparks, like what we just saw, it was a magical bug. But I'm going to tweak the spell a little." Nate reached toward the tiny hammer, and it settled in his palm again.

He repeated the incantation, adding:

> *Let truth be spoken, guilt be shown:*
> *The listener's name is hereby known.*

"There. That should take care of it and should also let me know who is responsible for eavesdropping on you." The hammer floated around the room once more before moving through the archway into the next room.

On silent feet, Olivia approached from the side door and stood next to Nate. "It's interesting that Malone is now a vampire. I've reached out to a council member for support in identifying his maker."

They keep talking, but they're not saying a fucking thing about finding Faith. Will I have to do this on Mickey's terms? On my own?

"WHAT'S the plan to find Faith?" Arlan asked, amazed that Nate hadn't led with that.

Nate pressed his finger to his lips and pointed to his ear.

Oh. He's clearing the listening devices first. Smart. Arlan nodded.

Dazed, Dinah shifted and stepped toward the table.

Arlan pulled out a chair for her.

Olivia moved toward Dinah, her lips moving as she

moved her arm in front of her. Writing appeared in the space between Dinah and Olivia.

We're waiting to talk about finding Faith until all the listening devices and spells have been destroyed. We don't want them to know our next move. Nod your head if you understand.

Dinah nodded, her eyes wide.

Olivia swiped a hand through the words hanging in the air. She repeated the process.

We know this is really hard for you—but you need to keep yourself together so we can find her as soon as possible. We have people on this already. We WILL get her back.

Dinah nodded again, seeming to relax slightly.

Olivia erased the last message before moving next to Dinah and wrapping an arm around her shoulders.

Arlan used his connection with the witches.

What are our next steps? I feel useless and don't know what I should be doing.

Nate looked him in the eye and nodded toward Dinah.

She needs you right now. You'll be her rock through this.

Arlan nodded, stepping toward Dinah and squatting in

front of her, in her line of sight. He grasped her hands and held them, sending every ounce of support and determination he could through his fingertips.

Between them, the air thickened and a faint pink glow washed over their hands. In his mind, he saw Dinah's heart—part of it broken away in the middle of a dark space. Through the connection, he sent her all the love he could muster. The room brightened—swirls of green and yellow filled the room and he sensed hope increasing with each passing moment.

Dinah palmed his cheek, directing him to face her, and their eyes met.

The unspoken words of love.

The anguish in her heart.

The fury that Mickey Malone would deign to steal away Faith.

And the determination to find that fucker and make sure he paid for Dinah's years of fear.

"The house is clear. Dinah, is it okay if we bring in a few members of our coven?"

The spell caster for all the devices was Gabriel Vincent. That name isn't familiar to me.

Dinah blinked, the moment with Arlan broken. "Whatever it takes to find Faith and bring her safely home. I don't care if we have every mystical Being in Michigan in my kitchen." She stood and moved to the sink, filling the coffee maker with water to put on a pot. "I don't have a lot in the way of refreshments—I can make...."

Olivia interrupted, "You do what you're comfortable

doing—or nothing at all. I can whip up anything we might need, dear. Your job is to focus on finding Faith."

"I know you're trying to keep your hands busy, but what if we write a list of places in Michigan you've known Mickey to frequent? I don't think he'll take her far—at least, not initially." Arlan kept his voice soft, concealing his own fear and anger.

"Maybe later. That's a very passive activity and I need to move right now," Dinah said.

"Dinah, how would you feel about a member of the council who happens to be a vampire coming to help us?" Olivia asked.

She spun around, fists pressed to her hips and elbows out to the side. "Why would you do that?"

Nate said, his voice gentle, "They're not all like him. The vampires here in Zephyr keep their virus under control with a carefully formulated compound that helps them stay nourished, so they don't devolve into the angry, predatory version you've seen in movies."

"'Carefully formulated compound?' What's in it?" Arlan asked.

"Think about it like a nutrition shake—only they're specifically for vampires," Olivia responded.

"I'll press this issue another time." He grinned before his expression turned somber. "Because right now, time is ticking away and the more time that passes, the lower the chances are that we'll find Faith."

A knock sounded at the door.

"Dinah, that's our friend from the council. Can he join us?" Olivia asked, her voice soft.

"Oh, yes. Sure. If he'll help find Faith—and wants to end Mickey Malone." Fire danced in her eyes as the desire for vengeance took over. Gone was the sad mother whose main reason for living for seventeen years had been her daughter, abducted by a piece-of-shit father. Her hard expression bolstered Arlan's belief that they'd find Faith and a soft cobalt glow formed around Dinah.

She strode to the side door and swung it open wide. "Hello. Welcome to my home. Please come in so we can get my daughter back."

This dude *looked* like a vampire. Stereotypical prominent widow's peak, pale skin, unique eyes, and he commanded the room as though he'd had centuries of practice.

"You don't have to invite me in. That's a fallacy. But it's the polite thing to do, anyway." He extended his right hand. "Roland Keen. You might know my son, Marc." He grinned, a sheepish expression replacing his dominance. "My spouse, Orlando, usually takes care of school things for the children. I suppose I should take a more active role, but he likes doing it."

Teacher Dinah emerged. "As long as someone at home knows what's going on at school, that's all that matters." She smiled, then startled. "Oh, I didn't mean to say you don't know what's going on. I'm sure Orlando—"

"Dinah. Dinah, it's fine. I knew what you meant." He smiled—his teeth appeared normal. "Our major focus is finding your daughter and discovering how this man came to be a vampire. As you know, the virus is transmittable through saliva—so the bite thing tracks, still." He paused, looking at her expectantly.

"Oh, I'm sorry. Everyone else is in the kitchen." She swung her arm toward her guests. "Can I get you anything?"

Roland placed his hand on her shoulder. "No, thank you. I need us to find your daughter. That is my only priority right now."

She relaxed minutely. "Good, because pretending to be fine takes entirely too much energy." Dinah pivoted and walked into the kitchen, into Arlan's arms.

As Nate, Olivia, and Roland talked in hushed tones, Dinah held tight to Arlan as her rapid breathing slowed and she relaxed even more. Finally, she turned and said, "Let's find this motherfucker and get Faith home—where she belongs."

chapter fourteen

More than an hour later, Dinah's frustration over waiting reached a point where she couldn't sit around anymore. *I know everyone is doing their best, but doing nothing is not working for me.* She looked out the kitchen window. "Children abducted by non-custodial parents make up ninety percent of missing children. The first three hours are the most critical."

"We know, Dinah. That's why we're getting a plan in place as quickly as possible. Something like this hasn't been on our radar before, so it's taking a minute." Nate sighed. "And we're not completely sure where to look."

"I don't know how much help it would be for me to make a list of places from seventeen years ago, but it's at least something I can do."

With a map of Michigan pulled up on her laptop, the catalog of Mickey's old haunts was long—for someone with such dubious business practices, he got around. Dinah recalled him bragging about all his connections in Chicago, Detroit, Grand Rapids, and Lansing—as well as Flint and Saginaw—before speaking in hushed tones about villages with small populations in remote areas with associates when he hadn't thought she was paying attention.

She always paid attention—even more so once she decided she needed to leave him.

"I don't know whether this will be helpful information or not, but it's at least something," Dinah said as she handed a paper with handwritten notes to Roland. *And it makes me feel like I'm contributing.*

"This is a place to start—for sure. Orlando's been online connecting with some of our clutch. The kids'll be getting up soon, but they're old enough to know what's going on."

"Oh, I think I'd appreciate it if we didn't mention this to Faith's classmates—or any school-aged children," Dinah said.

"Can I ask why?" Roland asked.

Arlan interjected, "First, knowing about magical Beings is different from needing help, and her abduction could be viewed as a weakness. Second, this is Dinah's business, and her students don't need to know about it. It could impact her relationship with them in numerous ways—even though we'd like to think that's not the case."

Dinah patted his arm. "The fact that Faith is only just meeting her sperm donor could also be viewed negatively by some students who might feel I was keeping her from him all this time without knowing all the details—which are absolutely inappropriate to get into with students. I hope you understand," she said.

Roland nodded. "That makes sense. Orlando will handle it—but we're typically quite active and involved with the kids all weekend. He'll get questions—especially from Marc."

"Marc will understand, I'm sure. He's very perceptive and knows when he can and can't push for more information," Dinah said.

Olivia looked at her phone. "We've got a lead. Mickey's been sighted at a warehouse on the other side of Petoskey. There are five or six people with him, according to our source," Olivia blurted out, excitement causing her voice to pitch higher.

Dinah's eyes stung with held-back tears. She turned away from the group and took a few deep breaths, calming her racing heart and schooling her immediate instinct to rush out and get Faith.

I know I need to be patient. It's so hard. If we screw up the plan, it could be very bad for Faith.

Her phone pinged—the "unknown" sound she'd assigned.

The coffee she'd had earlier sat in her stomach like a rock—but roiling like a violent storm on Lake Michigan at the same time.

> Caroline is safe. She's settling into my
> temporary housing solution very nicely.

He included a picture of Faith, bound to a chair in what appeared to be an office space.

She showed the image to Nate. "Is this office where you think they are?"

Nate enlarged the picture and looked it over. "Quite possibly. This is good news."

Her heart thudded in her ears as she struggled to keep

the emotion out of her voice. "With this knowledge, what are the next steps?" Dinah looked from person to person.

"I think we need to assemble a team to extract her without too much bloodshed. While it would be completely understandable to end Mickey for this, it is not appropriate to slay those whose only crime is taking direction from an immoral individual with psychopathic tendencies," Roland added.

Olivia chimed in, "And that's part of our agreement between Beings—that we aren't overly harsh on those who are ordered to do things that might be morally gray or even downright horrible."

Dinah nodded. "Understood. Still, what's the next step? We need to keep moving forward."

Roland looked at his phone and announced, "Orlando's got a direct hit. One of our clutch is with Mickey and we have verification that Faith is with them. Mickey's apparently drugged her, though. So, we'll plan accordingly, because she can't help herself right now."

Excitement and a mother's instinct to protect her young thrummed through Dinah. "I'm ready to go. Tell me what to do." She stood tall with her hands on her hips, expecting someone to give her a role.

"You can ride along once we have a fully formed plan, but you're not going into the warehouse. It's too dangerous for you," Olivia said.

Dinah pinned her with a death stare. "Would you say that to Hannah?"

Olivia froze, and then her expression melted into consideration. "I suppose I wouldn't say it to Hannah because she can use magic to protect herself. How can you protect yourself from Mickey—an irrational vampire?"

Roland said, "I agree, Dinah. Dealing with an irrational vampire who doesn't have control of his virus is dangerous for a human. Mickey's natural inclination is to infect people with the vampirism virus as he feeds from them. He won't hesitate to expose you. And, I hate to say it, but he likely has no qualms about infecting Faith because he sees his life as a vampire superior to his human life."

"While I have a lot of questions, now is not the time. So, I think a good solution is for Dinah and me to ride along and we'll stay with the vehicles—but at least one witch goes so I can be connected to what's going on and relay the information to Dinah," Arlan offered.

Nate nodded. "That seems reasonable—and I'm going, anyway. Faith will need someone she knows and trusts there when we free her."

"Mickey may have retained more of his human qualities than you give him credit for." Dinah paced in the small kitchen. "He's patient, crafty, and always thinking three steps ahead of anyone he perceives as an enemy. I wouldn't be surprised if he suspects we'll easily find him and is preparing for a major showdown to demonstrate his strength."

She turned, facing the people in the room who were ready to fight for her daughter. "We need to be prepared for that."

Nate said, "We've got a pretty large group on call who are readying for battle as though they're a brood—a sort-of family unit of vampires. This is the first time in a while we've had to do something like this, so it's taking a little more organization—but with everyone working together, we'll get there fast."

Roland added, "And with someone on the inside, we'll have the advantage."

"What if your mole is actually on Mickey's side and is trying to lure us there?" Arlan asked.

"Arlan. Don't think that way. We must take everything at face value until we have a reason to believe otherwise." Olivia cast a silent spell to straighten the papers strewn about the table.

Nate announced, "The plan is in place and the teams think they're ready to roll on our signal." He turned to Dinah. "Get some water and snacks for Faith. After she wakes up from whatever drug they used on her, she'll need lots of fluids and might be hungry." He looked at Arlan. "Get a blanket—something that washes up easily—not the ratty thing she sleeps with."

Olivia piped in, "Nate, don't tell the girl's secrets."

The man smiled, but it didn't reach his eyes. Etched with worry, Nate continued relaying the plan. "Roland, the shifters and witches have coordinated with Amber Newman, who has all of your people ready."

"That's what I'm hearing. All told, we're taking over sixty individuals and there are strategic plans in place." Roland added, "I need to swing home before we head out, so I'll see you there." He put his hand on Dinah's shoulder. "We've got at least one person to protect her, Dinah. She'll be safe until we can get there."

"Thanks, Roland." *Hopefully, we haven't underestimated Mickey and his influence over people.*

"I'VE NEVER SEEN you this stressed out. Believe me, this isn't happening again if I can help it," Arlan said as Dinah paced behind the vehicles about half a mile from the warehouse.

She paused, staring at him. "I should hope so. If there had been something we could have done to prevent it in the first place, that would've been absolutely fantastic." Dinah rolled her eyes and resumed her pacing.

She's hurt and worried about Faith—and Faith has been her world for nearly two decades.

Arlan, we're in the woods surrounding the warehouse.

Thanks, Nate. I'll let her know.

He reached into the open back end of the Equinox and pulled out two bottles of water. On Dinah's next pass past him, he offered her a bottle. "They're in place. Drink this. Can't have you dehydrated or overheating."

She snagged the bottle out of his hand, turning away from him as she paused to open it and drank a long pull. After a moment, she turned toward him. "I'm sorry I snapped. I am truly grateful you think enough of Faith and me to be so protective—and I absolutely believe you'd move mountains for her to be safe at home with us, watching *Charmed*. I guess now we'll pick it apart when we see something that isn't authentic." She smiled weakly.

Arlan pulled Dinah into his arms and put his chin on top of her head as she nestled in. "This is going to be new for us both. Actually, all three of us. It's been you and Faith for so long, I think that'll be the biggest adjustment: making room for me."

"I don't think it'll be difficult at all. We're at a transition point, anyway. This is a good time for you to come into our lives. Faith'll start applying to colleges and universities this spring and will have visits throughout the summer in addition to a camp or two. And Mara won't feel the need to keep me occupied the entire time Faith is gone. She can be...."

"A lot?" Arlan asked.

Dinah nodded. "That's a great way to put it. A lot. It feels like she's constantly pumping me for information, too." She backed up a bit and looked into his eyes. "Or maybe that's my perception, and it's how she shows interest in the lives of others."

She reached up and gave him a quick peck on the lips. "Thank you for distracting me. I was in my head, and I need to be present and positive. Soon, Faith will be back here, and she'll be fine."

It's a go. We're heading in.

Got it.

"They're entering the warehouse. Stick close to the car—once they're in and they have Mickey and his henchmen contained, Nate'll give me a signal and we'll drive up."

Dinah's eyes opened wide. "I thought they were going to bring her out here."

"I thought it'd be better if you were there as soon as possible."

Dinah threw her arms around his neck and squeezed him. "I'm so glad you're advocating for me and Faith. And I'm glad you're connected with Nate and Olivia so we can communicate without using technology." She released him and stepped backward. "Do you think we should get in the car to wait so we're ready once we receive word?" She turned toward the vehicle.

Arlan put a hand on her forearm. "Hey, breathe. First, let the team secure the area and make sure it's safe for us. No sense in getting ourselves in over our heads—this way, the team can do their job and not worry about us being in the way."

"You're right. You're right—I hate feeling useless."

"Enough of that." His voice served up a side order of reproach to go along with his words. "You have done an amazing job keeping her safe from Mickey. It was bound to happen at some point. At least you knew right away and have contacts who can help immediately."

"Oh, shit. What if she had been at school and no one realized she was missing?" Dinah gasped, a hand fluttered to her mouth, and she pressed her lips together as though she were swallowing down a cry.

"Hey, it didn't work out that way. And if it had? She has classmates that would have noticed and let someone know. Remember, we don't know the extent of the gifts and talents of our co-residents in Zephyr."

Dinah nodded. "You're right. I'd planned to show her pictures and go over all of this with her during our end-of-year break."

"Well, that's one less thing you have to do, isn't it?" Arlan grinned.

"Yup. It is. Hopefully, we'll know where Mickey is from now on."

"Hopefully. That'd certainly be nice. But I want you to

be prepared for the possibility that he'll escape. Or maybe he'll die, choosing not to back down."

"Good. The bastard took enough from me. He doesn't deserve to live—and he doesn't deserve the time he gets to spend with Faith." She shrugged out of his arms and began pacing again.

Arlan, it's going well. We outnumber them roughly six to one. It should be easy for us to contain Mickey and retrieve Faith.

Thanks, Nate. Are you ready for us, then?

Dinah's probably pacing like a caged tiger.

She is.

Gimme a couple minutes. I'll reach out when it's completely clear. Need to make sure there aren't any sympathizers lurking. Also, tell her Gunnar Meyer is here. He's been infected with the virus but surrendered immediately. Seems like he's got it under control.

Thanks.

"Nate said they're going to make sure it's clear before calling us in. He also said that Gunnar Meyer is there and turned himself in. He's infected with the virus."

Dinah's lips trembled. "I— I don't know whether to be happy or sad about that."

"It's surely a lot to take in. Whatever your feelings, they're valid."

She nodded. "Something still feels off, though."

"A mother's intuition is some pretty powerful magic. We'll see what's up when we get there. Nate would warn us if you needed to prepare—"

Faith's definitely drugged. There's a partial vial of diazepam here. Have Dinah call Aaron Jepson—he knows what's going on—and find out if there's anything special we need to know or do right now.

Got it.

He relayed the information to Dinah.

"That bastard." She pulled out her cell and found the number for Doctor Jepson, then reached for Arlan's phone.

"They've got Mickey. You could probably use your phone."

She shook her head. "What if someone is still tracking it? Not worth the risk."

"Smart." He handed over his device.

Dinah punched in the number and put it on speaker once the call connected.

"Doctor Jepson."

"Aaron, it's Dinah James."

"Ah, shit. What's going on, Dinah? Is Faith okay?"

"They said she's unconscious and drugged—there's a vial of diazepam. Anything we need to know?"

Silence. "Depends on how much he gave her."

"All I know is 'partially empty' according to Nate."

"Watch for blue lips, fingernails, and skin as well as trouble breathing. I'll meet you at your house. Let me know when you're on your way back."

"Will do. See you soon." She disconnected the call and gave Arlan his phone back.

Worry etched lines in her forehead, between her brows, and pinched her lips.

"I know telling you not to worry is likely to land poorly, so I'm not doing that. But I think things have ended up better than the original plan indicated."

"How so?" Dinah asked.

"They neutralized the brood quickly and with zero casualties on either side. That's always a good thing."

Dinah growled. "Better than originally planned wouldn't have my daughter drugged into unconsciousness."

"I know, I know. But this is a better case than some we'd planned for."

Wide-eyed, Dinah gasped. "What was the worst-case scenario, then?"

Arlan looked at her. "Dinah...."

"No, just say it. They planned for finding Faith dead or infected, didn't they." Her eyes darted around the open space.

"They did have to plan for those outcomes, but strongly suspected she'd be just fine because Mickey wouldn't want to harm his daughter."

"Well, it's a good thing I wasn't there for this planning, then."

Arlan nodded. "I only got the brief version. I never for one second thought Mickey would harm her or infect her."

You can bring Dinah. We're getting Faith to the entrance. She's out cold.

"Let's go get our girl."

chapter fifteen

They crested another hill just as the sun started to peek out over the horizon.

This drive is taking forever.

Sure she'd misunderstood how far they were from the warehouse, Dinah looked forward, leaning to see inches further as she waited for the turn that would take her to her daughter.

"Almost there. Nate's saying she's breathing fine, and her pulse is okay. There's an EMT with them."

Dinah sighed. "That's something. I still need to see her with my own eyes, though."

Arlan nodded. "I get it. I'm a little eager to see her myself." He reached his arm across the console and put his palm on her thigh, calming the bouncing. "I can't imagine what must've gone through your head during this entire thing."

Damn straight you can't imagine. She reigned in the thought. *He truly cares.* "This was my worst nightmare, fulfilled. But knowing Nate's got everything under control helps. I know it's been hard on you, too. You and Faith have developed quite the bond over the past month or so. And I realize she also cares about you—that I'm not the only major influence in her life anymore."

"She's got both Nate and Olivia—and Hannah—as positive influences. They care about you and Faith so much. I hope you've not felt alone all this time," Arlan said.

"I've tried to let people in to share my feelings, but it's so difficult when everything's been such a secret until now." Dinah gasped. "Is that the driveway? Is it?"

Arlan chuckled. "It is, my lovely." He maneuvered the Equinox into the pot-holed driveway and across asphalt as pockmarked as Swiss cheese.

Around the back of the building, a small group congregated. Zip ties restrained some individuals, while others bore metal shackles.

"We're going to the second loading dock. The first one has men who kill high-school girls for sport."

She didn't ask for clarification; the less she knew, the better.

Spotting Olivia a hundred yards ahead of them, standing in front of a loading bay door, Dinah took a deep breath.

Arlan stopped and barely had the transmission in "park" before Dinah swung open the door and ran up to Olivia, scouring the area for signs of Faith.

"Dinah. Stop. Breathe." Olivia smoothed her palm up and down Dinah's upper arm.

"Don't give me that. You haven't had your child kidnapped by a vampire who happened to be their sperm donor." Then she spotted her.

Nate cradled Faith in his arms, her head tucked under his chin.

Time paused and Dinah froze, seemingly secured to the spot where she stood. Using deep breaths, she slowed her heart rate until the organ felt like it would remain in her chest for a little longer. With a final deep inhale, she jogged over to meet Nate.

Callie Hersch, the EMT, said, "Ms. James, she's stable. We'll want Doc Jepson to take a look at her, but I'm sure she'll be fine. Once the drugs are out of her system, she'll be back to normal."

Dinah chuckled. "Hardly normal. She's learned a lot in the past twenty-four hours and her life is likely to never be the same."

Callie grinned. "Of that, I'm sure. I'm a coyote shifter—I'd always wanted to tell you while I was in school. It was pretty hard to write some of your papers without adding Being history."

"I'm going to put her in the back seat of your car," Nate said. "Did you want to get the door for me and slide in the back to help get her settled?"

Dinah said, "Yes—thank you." She turned to Callie again. "And thanks for sharing and taking care of Faith, Callie." She jogged over to Arlan and Olivia, interrupting their conversation. "Ready to go?"

He nodded and immediately rounded the Equinox and slid behind the steering wheel.

Dinah opened the back door before she slipped around the hood, getting into the passenger-side, second-row seat.

Nate placed Faith into the vehicle and stabilized her until Dinah had settled.

Faith's skin was clammy, and she slept deeply—like she had as an infant.

"I'll call Doc and let him know you're on the way," Nate said. "There's no hurry, so drive carefully."

Dinah rolled her eyes. *My child's health will always be an emergency for me.*

"Dinah, I mean it. She's fine—just has to get the medication they used on her out of her system. Doc might be able to help with that."

Callie said, "I sent a picture of the drug bottle and syringe used to Doc. We need to leave this stuff in place for the police."

"Thanks." Arlan turned toward her. "You all set back there?"

Dinah had wrapped the blanket they'd brought around Faith. Dinah stroked her hair as she cradled Faith's head in her lap. "Yes." Her heart pounded, and she rested a palm on Faith's back, measuring the rise and fall of her chest as she took slow breaths.

She's breathing. It never crossed her mind that Faith wouldn't survive—she was, after all, schooled in what to do should she ever be in this type of situation. Dinah had impressed upon her skills based on all the latest research about abductions—especially those by non-custodial parents. Faith's only job was to say what she had to in order to stay alive.

Faith shifted, inhaled deeply, and exhaled. A smile appeared on her face, which morphed from the cherubic adorableness of a Botticelli to that of a young, powerful woman ready to take on the world. With Frida Kahlo's intensity, Amelia Earhart's tenacity, and Mary Shelley creativity, Faith was ready to make her mark.

With all fears of Mickey Malone behind them, joy spread through her chest and threatened to bubble out through her lips. Pressing them together to tamp back emotions, she relaxed enough to say, "Thank you for being here for us, Arlan."

"There's nowhere else I'd rather be." He glanced over his shoulder and then into the rear-view mirror, seeming to stare into her eyes.

They stayed like that, Arlan's focus flicking back and forth between the road and the rearview, for what seemed like an eternity before the corners of his eyes crinkled and his cheeks bunched in a smile. Then he returned his attention to driving.

Focused on Faith's breathing and taking in the reality that she was there, basically unharmed, Dinah's sense of calm was restored.

Arlan will keep us safe.

He loves us.

Mickey Malone is no longer a threat.

WHILE ARLAN FOCUSED on arriving at Dinah's home as fast as possible, his mind wandered.

How did the team that went in corral the vampires and win them over?

What does it take to kill a vampire?

Arlan, we have a problem.

Nate's voice in his head echoed around, and the sinking feeling in his gut intensified.

I'm listening.

Mickey is missing. We had him in enchanted handcuffs and leg irons, but he managed to escape. We're on our way to you —if you can, slow down so we can catch up.

Got it.

Oh, Arlan? I wouldn't mention this to Dinah.

That's a bad idea, Nate.

Your call. I think she'll overreact. It's likely that Mickey is leaving the area and will regroup at some point. For now, he's a rogue vampire without a brood or clutch—and it makes him vulnerable.

"Hey, babe? There's a slight problem. Mickey escaped the magical shackles and is missing."

"I figured this would happen. Our primary concern is getting home, so Doc Jepson can take a look at Faith. We'll think about where Mickey is and what he's doing later." Her voice was flat—nothing like that of the passionate woman he knew.

What's going on with her? Is this a parent thing?

"Nate thought the same—glad you two have similar thoughts."

"Mmhm." She turned away, looking out the window instead of in the rearview.

"You okay back there?" he asked.

"Yup." She looked into the rearview again. "Why do you ask?"

"You seem…distant. Is it something I did?"

Dinah smiled. "No. I'm trying to not freak out because my daughter's been drugged, and Mickey is still at-large. I need to keep it together until I know she's okay. Then, I'll have a little fall apart to get it out of my system before I focus on getting Faith past this and the trauma she endured."

"I wondered if it was a parent thing."

"Arlan, if you did something, I'd tell you right away. I'm too old to play games and you deserve better than that." She glanced downward before raising her gaze once again. "I'm sorry I've gotten you wrapped up in this. I always wondered whether he was keeping tabs on me, and it looks like he was. So much so that I wonder who his mole in Zephyr is. It's gotta be someone who knows us fairly well. Mickey has been able to get my number any time I've changed it. Sometimes it takes him a year or two to catch up, but he's never far."

"How does that make you feel?" he asked.

"I'm always waiting for him to do something. To be truthful, I expect him to strike within a week. Knowing someone else bested him—captured him, even though he managed to somehow escape—won't sit well with his over-inflated ego."

Arlan nodded.

She continued, "And if he's as well connected as he was when we were together, it'll only take hours for him to organize another team. They might not be his first choice, but they'll have sworn fealty to him and will have vowed to protect him at all costs. It's how he keeps his hands clean."

"There's a brood of vampires in Petosky—I overheard him talking with a small group on the other side of the warehouse." Faith's hoarse whisper was the best sound he'd heard all day.

"Hey, baby. How're you feeling?" Dinah asked Faith.

"I'm okay," she said weakly.

"We're on the way home and Doc Jepson will meet us there to get you looked at," Dinah said.

"'kay." The partial word had a tone of finality. "Gonna sleep more."

"Rest. I'm here and nothing will ever happen again, as long as we're together."

The determined set of her jaw scared Arlan. *Will she refuse to allow Faith to go to school? What about Faith's dreams? And what does this mean for us?*

The thoughts rolled around in his head, and they traveled in silence until they arrived at the turnoff to Dinah's home.

I need to learn how to protect them—keep them safe.

We're right behind you. Go ahead and park in the driveway. Back in so the passenger side is closest to the door in case there are nosey neighbors.

Plus, that sets us up for a quick escape.

A few neighbors were outside, watching for them. Annika Pope's mother waved and started walking down the sidewalk toward the house.

Doc Jepson is parked on the street—I see him standing next to his car. Carly Pope is walking toward the house, too.

Carly's going to throw up a glamour spell so no one can see the activity going on around Dinah's property.

Got it.

"When we get home, no one will be able to tell from the outside what's going on—Carly Pope is going to use magic to do that."

"That sounds complicated—she must be pretty powerful. I can't believe I never knew there were Beings in Zephyr. It seems so clear to me now," Dinah said.

"Hopefully, I'll be able to learn spells like that soon," Arlan replied.

She looked down at Faith again. "You will. There's a reason for you to know that stuff now."

Arlan pulled past Dinah's driveway and backed in after scrutinizing the area, ensuring there were no signs of Mickey or anyone else.

"We're going to wait until Nate gets here and gives us the 'all clear' to get out of the vehicle." Arlan glanced toward the street. "He's parking right now."

Aaron Jepson stood next to the car, an aura of bronze and lilac swirling around him, giving Arlan extra patience and calmness.

Arlan turned and reached into the back seat.

Dinah grasped his hand. "This is going to work out. I know it." An orange filter spread between them.

He said, "I think so—I've studied color theory and I'm

noticing auras around people now that equates to the theoretical qualities in a person."

"That's interesting. I can feel a person's intentions a little more intensely than I could before. I wonder if you're able to amplify that or something."

He squeezed her hand and then released her. "Maybe. I've got a lot to learn about my powers."

Once Nate stood next to Doc Jepson, Arlan turned off the vehicle and Nate opened the back door, reaching for Faith.

"Honey, we're home. Papa Nate is going to help you inside."

Arlan whipped the door open, slammed it shut, and raced around the back of the SUV to unlock the door. When he reached out with the key, a glittering sphere floated between his hand and the lock. He heard a *click*, and the knob turned before the door swung open.

"Don't stand there slack-jawed. Get Dinah inside. We'll be in Faith's room." Nate delivered the line with a chuckle.

"Got it," Arlan said.

"Once you're in with the door locked, bring Faith water and a snack." The doctor's voice was light—as though this were something that happened every day.

"Yes, sir." Arlan nodded, then reached into the Equinox to extract Dinah. "Let's go, baby."

Dinah scooted across the bench seat and into Arlan's arms.

"To Faith's room—like Doc Jepson said. I'll get us all water and bring some decent nibbles." He pulled open the storm door, holding it for Dinah.

"Thank you—for everything." Tears welled in her eyes.

"You don't have to thank me. I wish this'd never happened in the first place."

chapter sixteen

Three hours later, Dinah sat in the rocker in Faith's room watching her sleep, Mac in her lap.

Before Doc Jepson left, she'd been awake and alert, drank a bottle of water, and eaten some cheese cubes and pretzels. He'd said Faith would likely doze on and off for the rest of the day.

Once she'd known Faith would be fine, she'd refocused on the threat of Mickey Malone and what his next step might be.

She rose, cradling Mac, and settled him on Faith's bed before she crept out of her daughter's room, leaving the unicorn plushies and mermaid wall hangings which stood in sharp contrast to the *Rent* and *Hamilton* posters on the adjacent surface.

"Hey. You ready for some dinner?" Arlan asked.

She nodded. "What time is it?" she asked as his arms wrapped around her, and she settled into the comfortable spot under his chin.

"It's almost five and you've not had anything significant today. I hope you don't mind, but I pulled some stuff out of the freezer and defrosted it."

"You're amazing," Dinah said as she leaned back a bit to look up at him.

Their lips met—a chaste brush of flesh—and contentment spread through Dinah's chest.

"Only because you're so prepared and have enough chicken breasts in there for at least two weeks' worth of meals," he said.

Nate came into the living room from the kitchen. "Oh, you've emerged. Good. I'm going to go sit with Faith for you. Relax." The older man's voice washed over her like a soothing balm.

"Thank you. I came out to stretch my legs. Plus, while her breathing is fascinating and I'm so grateful for it, it gets boring after a bit." Dinah chuckled.

On her way to Faith's room, he paused and wrapped his arms around both Dinah and Arlan, giving them a little squeeze. "This is under control. Relax." He patted her back before releasing and moving down the hallway and disappearing into Faith's room.

Melting back into Arlan, she whispered, "What's going on now?"

They swayed together for a few moments. Then he said, "The Three are warding the house right now. Carly's still holding the glamour so passersby can't see anyone on the property—nor additional vehicles in the street."

"Okay. Do we have any news as to Mickey's whereabouts?" she asked.

As if dancing to music, they moved toward the kitchen. "There are people on it—they're checking the towns you listed, but there are others looking for him in the area. If he's anywhere close, they'll track him down."

"How? I don't mean to sound like I don't believe things are being done—I just want to understan—"

"It's natural for you to have questions. Calvin Cook is an excellent tracker, and he's following Mickey with a detail of vampires accompanying him," Arlan said.

"Calvin? Really? That's interesting."

"Nate said he's the best. He doesn't get a lot of practice but tends to be able to hyper focus on something."

"Calvin is a mathematical genius and autistic. I heard he'll be working over at the new distillery beyond the subdivision north of town," Dinah said.

Arlan nodded. "He mentioned something about that."

"You met him?"

"Yup—he stopped here before he went to the warehouse to catch Mickey's scent. He's an opossum shifter. I found that interesting."

Dinah nodded. "Thinking back, it makes sense. He would freeze when he was overwhelmed when he was in my class. The academics never phased him, but scents were hard for him. I had to make sure I didn't change anything for the few years he was my student unless I pre-warned him."

"How so?"

Dinah paused. "He needed to know if I changed the air freshener scent or if the disinfectant wipes I used in the room were a different 'flavor.' He used flavor a lot when he talked about smells. I made sure the maintenance staff were aware of his sensory needs so we could let him know about changes. He did quite well in school—I think he was valedictorian of his class, if I remember correctly."

"Anyway, he's tracking Mickey and they're in Harbor Springs right now. They think he might have a boat docked there and need to get to him before he casts off."

"He'd always had an affinity for water. When he lived in Detroit, he had a sailboat he kept on Belle Isle."

"Good information," he said and then kissed her forehead before releasing her and reaching for his phone. He sent a text. "I notified the team. There isn't a witch with them—they're all nearby."

"Really? Why is that?"

"Nate said he'd feel better if the more senior members of the coven stayed back to support the Three."

"That's logical. I guess. From what I know about witchcraft—which is basically nothing." She chuckled.

"That makes two of us, but I'm learning." He moved toward the stove, lifted a lid from a pot, and swirled his finger in a circle.

"Did you just stir that with magic?"

Arlan smiled. "I did. Practice makes perfect, right?"

Dinah nodded. "That's true—that's what we say about test taking and math." She grinned. "Plus, I'm excited to see all the things you can do."

His light expression dimmed. "I wish I'd known sooner —I'd've been able to protect you and Faith better."

"It wouldn't have made any difference—you wouldn't have known. I was *just* toying with the idea of telling you when the texts started," Dinah said.

"Speaking of texts…it looks like Mara's sent you a few since we got back and switched your phone off airplane mode. You should check."

Dinah sighed and reached for the device on the kitchen

table. She unlocked it and a red circle rested over the message icon, a big ol' 12 centered in it. She tapped the chat bubble. "A dozen messages from Mara? Did she text you at all?"

Arlan shook his head.

She read through the missives and Mara's level of hippie calm decreased with successive texts.

> Dinah—I'm really worried. Let me know you're okay. If I don't hear from you by 6 pm, I'm coming over there.

Dinah checked the time. Half-past five.

> Hey. Sorry. We were doing stuff, and I didn't have my phone with me. We're fine. Why are you so worried?

> ...

The three dots appeared and then disappeared. And then, re-appeared.

> I just had a weird feeling. Glad all is well. Have a good night.

> You too. See you on Monday.

"Strange. She didn't ask about nor tease me about seeing you." Tension formed between her eyebrows.

"What did she want?"

"She said she had a weird feeling—but she's never confided that she gets premonitions. I'd believe her if she did. She has some definite otherworldly vibes."

Arlan shrugged as he pulled the chicken breasts from

the oven. He'd made a half dozen. "Can you get out a large colander so I can drain this pasta?" he asked.

Moving through the space, Dinah did as requested before getting out of the cooking area and leaning against the wall next to the window. "Anything else I can do to help?" she asked.

Arlan shook his head. "I think I've got it. Oh! You could toss a couple handfuls of spinach in the sauce there and stir, I guess. I'm going to put the sauce on the noodles in a minute."

"What's in this?" Dinah asked as she stirred the greenish cream-based mixture.

"It's a pesto Alfredo."

Dinah nodded. "Smells divine."

After draining the noodles, Arlan added the sauce and diced the chicken, stirring it into the concoction. He scooped some into three bowls. "Do you have a tray I can put together for Nate? I wanted to take him some. He's so kind to stick around."

Dinah pulled out a bed tray table from the skinny cabinet next to the stove. It folded, so the legs tucked inside the frame, and she loved using it for their hot chocolate and evening snacks. "This'll work." She set it on the table.

Arlan placed a bowl on the tray and then retrieved a cloth napkin from the drawer, along with silverware. "What do you think he'll want to drink?" he asked.

Dinah thought. "Normally, I'd say wine, but due to the situation, water."

He pulled a bottle from the refrigerator and placed it on the tray before picking it up. "Be right back. You can set the table if you want." He smiled and walked down the hallway.

She listened to his footsteps growing softer and softer. *He's so thoughtful. What did I do to deserve him?*

"MUMMA?" Faith said.

They'd fallen asleep on the couch after dinner.

Dinah shot up, almost colliding with Arlan's chin. "What? What? Are you okay?" She moved around the coffee table and swooped Faith into her arms.

The teen melted into her mother's embrace. "I'm fine. Just a bad dream."

Nate appeared from down the hallway. "I must've dozed off."

"I needed my mom, anyway, Papa." Faith sighed and snuggled closer to Dinah.

"You hungry?" Dinah asked.

Faith nodded.

"Arlan made pesto Alfredo and pasta with wilted spinach and chicken."

"Sounds yummy."

Dinah released her and the two separated, only to settle on the couch. She looked at Arlan, her expression an unspoken "Would you mind, darling?"

Arlan nodded, stood, kissed both Faith and Dinah on the forehead, and went into the kitchen to warm some dinner for Faith.

The clock on the microwave read 8:15 when he put the bowl inside and tapped the *1* button.

He took the time to check his cell.

> Still tracking, but we're stopping for dinner so Cal can keep going.

> Back at it. Nearly to Cross Village.

> Notifying people in the UP to possibly intercept.

Olivia walked in. "Good news. We have some state troopers in the upper peninsula who 'detained' Mickey on the north end of the Mackinac Bridge. They're transporting him to a facility maintained by the Beings. This one's designed to rehabilitate vampires and get them used to maintaining their health through the formula now available."

"That *is* good news," Arlan said. He pointed to the bowl of noodles, chicken, and sauce. "Hungry? There's plenty."

Olivia shook her head. "Maybe in a few minutes. Everyone in the living room?" He tipped his head toward the archway.

Nate appeared, gravitating to Olivia. He enveloped her in his arms.

They both relaxed. They separated, but their hands remained clasped.

"C'mon." He tugged her with him toward the living room.

Arlan followed.

"Mickey's been detained at a Being facility," Olivia announced.

"Good," Faith spat out.

"Listen, honey. They're going to try to rehabilitate him. Get him used to the synthetic nutrition we've developed. If he can prove he's no longer a threat to you, your mom, or society in general, he'll be released," Nate said.

Dinah shook her head. "I don't believe he can make that change. He was a threat even before he became a vampire."

"You'll have a chance to speak with the review board in charge of that before anything happens," Olivia said.

"That's good. So, now we can return to normal?" Arlan asked.

"Relatively. We still have the property warded and we'll want you to maintain those. We'll boost the wards at the school, so that's another safe zone." Nate paused.

"I don't like that look. What is it?" Dinah asked as she rose from the couch.

"Nothing major. We were talking, and we'd like Arlan to do a boot camp of sorts every weekend for the next three months or so. Get him quickly up to speed on his powers." He glanced at Olivia.

"I'll come stay with you here or you can come to our house. I know you might not feel all that comfortable being alone for a while." Olivia stepped toward Dinah and grasped her hand.

Arlan looked at each of them in turn: Dinah, Olivia, and then Nate. "What aren't you saying?"

Nate sighed. "Fine. We don't know if Mickey's brood—his 'family' of vampires—will come after him. We don't want you left alone and unprotected."

Dinah rolled her eyes. "Why didn't you say that in the first place?" She sighed. "Really, you can tell us what's going on. We deserve to know."

Nate extended a hand in front of him and faced his palm to the floor. He bounced it slightly as he said,

"Simmer down, firecracker. We don't want to keep things from you, but there's been a lot going on these past few days. Thought it might be a little overwhelming."

"Overwhelming to our human minds?" Faith asked.

Nate rolled his eyes. "Not the way you're thinking. We wanted you and your mom and Arlan to focus on your recovery from your abduction before we got into the longer-term situation."

"That's fine and all—but I think we'd rather know what's going on in real time," Dinah said, settling back into the couch.

Faith sat next to her, leaning into Dinah. Mac joined the pair, settling in Faith's lap. She stroked his long fur absently.

"Right now, you're safe here and will be safe at the school by Monday. Any witch that's warded their property against intruders will be a safe place—that's most of us. We're going to get Arlan caught up so you're all set and can regain a little independence. He'll be able to eventually put a bubble of sorts around you that will sound an alarm for him if any Beings approach; he'll even be able to sort the types of Beings he'll be notified about. This'll keep you safe from Mickey's brood until we can bring them all in. Those who were at the warehouse are cooperating and voluntarily getting the help they need to keep their virus under control." Olivia looked at Nate.

He nodded.

"In the meantime—and I know you two aren't going to take this well—we think it's best that you only go to school, our house, and back home. We'll get groceries, takeout, fancy coffee—whatever you need—until we've got a handle on this," Olivia said.

"I'm too exhausted to think about this right now," Dinah said.

"Understandable. I'm going to stay here tonight so you all can get some rest," Olivia replied.

"And I'll be here, too," Nate added.

Faith perked up. "Family sleep-over! Can Kennedy come over?" She looked from Dinah to Olivia and back.

Dinah waved her hand. "Whatever Olivia says is fine. But you need to eat your dinner, and then I think we can watch one episode of *Charmed* before calling it a night."

"Let's hold off until next weekend for that. You can all stay at our house," Olivia said.

Faith ate dinner.

Dinah made cocoa.

Charmed played, and Olivia and Nate chuckled at some of the happenings in the show.

Finally, Dinah tucked Faith in, and Olivia melted into the rocker in the corner of the room. Mac curled into Faith, keeping a protective eye out for any ne'er-do-wells.

Nate settled in on the couch with the remote, flipping through channels.

Dinah and Arlan sequestered themselves in Dinah's room.

Cuddled together in bed, Dinah snuggled into Arlan, draping an arm and a leg across him. When her breathing slowed and her tense muscles relaxed, Arlan gave in to sleep.

chapter seventeen

"Dinah! Daaaarrrrrling! You look simply fabulous," Mara drawled.

"Thanks. I'm trying something different." Instead of dressing to blend into the background, Dinah attempted to embrace how she felt: vibrant, full of life, and ready to conquer the world. She no longer had to hide in the shadows to ensure she and Faith remained safe.

With the help of Mickey's brood from the warehouse, a team of Beings rounded up the remaining associated vampires who all voluntarily went into treatment.

Mickey accepted help and was working through the phases to fully integrate the nutrition element—although he still maintained he would find Dinah and his daughter. He would not be released until he proved he wasn't a threat to anyone. His therapist thought he might eventually get there, but it'd be a while.

And Dinah and Arlan had gone public about their relationship. After some good-natured ribbing from some of the students, the novelty wore off and everything was back to normal.

Well, as normal as it could be with a partner who had newly developed magical powers he enjoyed practicing regularly.

And Dinah didn't mind one bit that he practiced by cleaning her house, folding her laundry, and doing her yard work.

It gave them more time to spend together.

Faith blossomed under her newfound freedom. Since Dinah no longer had to worry about Mickey finding them, she'd given Faith permission to travel with friends and even take the car into Petoskey—sometimes as far as Harbor Springs. With reasonable limits, of course.

Faith also enjoyed exploring social media—something Dinah didn't understand.

"Well, emerald is *definitely* your color. Put it on your 'get more of this' list!"

Arlan came around the corner as the two women walked down the hallway toward the teachers' lounge. "If it isn't my favorite girl."

"Why, Mr. DeSalvo! You make me blush," Mara said.

Dinah slapped her arm. "Mara, you're incorrigible."

Mara curtsied. "I aim to please." She grinned. "Alas, I think I'm going to get myself some hot water and go back to my room to eat. I've got some work on a sample project to do, so I don't need to stay too late tonight."

"We'll miss you but understand. I'm sure there are other teachers who will talk to us."

Mara snort-laughed and quickly covered her mouth.

Dinah laughed, and Arlan joined her.

"Ta-ta, lovebirds!" Mara waved as she spun, and her many-colored skirt fluttered around her legs. She flounced down the hallway.

"We *could* go to my classroom, you know. We don't need to have a chaperone anymore," Arlan said.

"We *could* go back to mine, too." She waggled her eyebrows. "I've got a little couch and everything...."

"Maybe the lounge is a better idea—if we're alone, it'll be hard to keep my hands off you." Arlan leaned in and kissed her cheek.

"If you insist." She sighed dramatically.

"I do, as a matter of fact."

"Faith'll be at the last football game of the season tonight. I wasn't planning to go because it's too cold for me," Dinah said, her voice husky.

"I think I can keep you warm," Arlan murmured after glancing around.

"You've got yourself a deal," she said, slipping her hand into his.

The usual teachers, plus Faith, Mara, Janae, Nate, Olivia, Hannah, and Kennedy, stood inside the lounge when Arlan opened the door.

She looked from person to person. "I really hope you're not ambushing me for a fashion emergency—y'all could've just said something...."

They all laughed. Out of the corner of her eye, she caught a teacher with their cell phone trained on her. *Video recording? Oh, no...this better not be—*

"We all know that Dinah James has been an amazing teacher for the sixteen years she's been teaching at Zephyr Junior/Senior High School," Janae said.

Kelly McCoy cleared her throat. "That's why the entire faculty is excited to announce...."

"That you, Dinah James, have been voted faculty homecoming royalty," Arlan finished. "Sorry, that means you need to go to the game tonight." He grinned.

Applause surrounded her, and tears welled along her waterline. When the clapping subsided, she said, "Aw, thank you. It was an honor to have the students nominate me—but to have my peers vote for me? That's just amazing —and makes my day."

Nate and Olivia approached her.

"Now, make sure you take care of your voice so you can announce the entire homecoming court at the game," Nate quipped.

"I will." She turned to Arlan. "I'm glad this is all it was."

"Why? What did you *think* was going to happen?"

"Well, when I saw everyone in here, I thought you were going to...."

He pulled Dinah against him in a one-armed hug. "I can, one hundred percent, tell you that I will not propose to you in public. That's not who we are." He kissed her cheek again.

She leaned her head on his shoulder. "Good. Glad to hear it."

"But that doesn't mean you shouldn't be considering what your answer might be," he whispered. "I love you."

THAT EVENING, Dinah wore a thick forest green cloak, protecting her from the elements of the late-October night-time chill. Faith had been a member of the homecoming court the previous year, so Dinah knew the drill.

After announcing the court and the crowning, she returned to the bleachers to find Arlan.

He stood at the edge of the structure with their blanket, holding a Styrofoam cup. "Thought you might like some coffee."

Taking the beverage, she said, "Thank you. That's so thoughtful." Dinah gave him a peck on the cheek.

"Let's go," he said, and stuck out his elbow.

She threaded her free hand through the crook and sighed.

Arlan leaned toward her. "We're going out of town for the night."

"Arlan, I can't—"

"You'll be back before noon and have plenty of time to help Faith get ready for the dance."

"But Faith—"

"Faith has the car, and she's going to spend the night with Kennedy."

"How—"

"I know you, Dinah James. But if you don't want to take a sexy overnight getaway...."

"Mr. DeSalvo, if I didn't know better, I'd swear you were trying to seduce me."

"Oh, Ms. James. I definitely *am* trying to seduce you."

They reached the black Prius and Arlan opened the passenger-side door and held Dinah's coffee as she settled in the seat.

She took it and said, "Thank you for the surprise. It's been one of those days."

Once he settled in the driver's seat, he said, "And how do you feel about surprises?"

"Historically, I haven't been a fan. But now? I think I could get used to them."

"Good. Because I had Faith pack you a bag. Now, turn your phone off."

"But—"

"If there's an emergency, Faith, Hannah, Kennedy, or Nate will contact me."

"Fine, but I'm going to send Faith a text first, letting her know."

"If you must. But beware. She was totally on board with my plan."

Dinah cast a sidelong glance at Arlan, taken in by the sparkle in his eye as he grinned like a Cheshire cat, his face only illuminated by the dashboard light.

Heading out with Arlan until tomorrow. But you knew that already. Love you. Have fun with Kennedy.

LOL Mom. YOU have fun. Can't wait to see you once you get home. LMK when you're on your way.

Will do.

She powered down her phone and slid it into her purse. "There. You happy?"

His grin was broad. "Yes. Absolutely. This is the first time you've been wholly mine."

"That's not true, an—"

"You are always 'on' via phone for Faith. That is not an option right now, is it."

"I guess. I mean, it's hard to believe we're safe from Mickey."

Arlan nodded. "And if Mickey shows up, *I* can protect you. Nate said I know enough protection spells and wards to ensure our safety, should the need arise—which is why I have the weekend off from bootcamp."

"Is *that* why we're going out of town?" Dinah asked.

"Partially. I've got a lot planned for the next twelve hours."

"Care to share, Mr. DeSalvo?" she asked.

"Not at this time, Ms. James." He grinned again.

They stopped at the sign when they came to US 31 and turned right.

"Are we going to the Dark Sky Park?"

"Nope."

"Would you tell me if I guessed correctly?"

"Nope."

She sighed. "I'm sort-of new at this 'surprises' shit, you know," she ground out.

"Yup." He grinned.

"You're enjoying this, aren't you."

"Mmhm." He nodded.

"Why doesn't that surprise me?"

"Nothing about me should surprise you anymore. Not really."

"Fine. But I still think we have things to learn about one another."

Arlan shifted toward her briefly, before refocusing on the road. "Oh, definitely."

"As long as we're in agreement."

"We are."

"Hey, Siri. Play The Best Damn Playlist for Dinah."

"Playing The Best Damn Playlist for Dinah," the mechanical voice said over the automobile speakers.

"You made me a playlist?" Dinah asked.

"Mmhm."

"That's so sweet of you."

"Nothing sweet about it. I was thinking about you, and I put together a bunch of songs that remind me of you."

Stevie Wonder sang the first song. *You Are the Sunshine of My Life.* A favorite of Dinah's since her teen years. "This song won the Grammy for Best Male Pop Vocal Performance in 1973."

"You never fail to surprise me." He reached over the console, found her hand, and laced their fingers together.

"My mom used to listen to Stevie Wonder a lot," she said.

"I didn't know. You mentioned she died when you were young."

"Yes. I was seven. My dad tried, but I spent a lot of time with my aunts—especially once I hit puberty."

Arlan sang along with the lyrics for a few moments.

Dinah fell a little harder for him with each note he sang.

Next on the list, "Wonderful Tonight" by Eric Clapton.

"Why did you pick this one?" she asked.

"You always look wonderful to me, so I wanted to make sure this was on the list—to remind you." Arlan squeezed her hand.

The next song—"Against All Odds" by Phil Collins—was also a favorite.

"I know why this one is on the list. After Mickey kidnapped Faith and we were finally able to be together in public, I played this all the time—because it seemed like we were together, even in the face of adversity."

He nodded. "My thoughts exactly."

They rode in silence until the next song began and Dinah exclaimed, "I am not perfect."

"But listen to the lyrics. It's us. Sheeran could've been secretly recording our relationship thus far."

"I guess. But I really hate the term 'perfect.'"

"Noted." And then Arlan sang along with Ed.

"I don't think I've ever heard you sing—you have a lovely voice," Dinah said.

"Thanks. I wish you'd cut loose and sing along. I know you know the words," Arlan murmured.

"I will, but I'm enjoying listening to you."

"You'll know the next one. I've heard you say how much you love it, and I've seen you chair dancing when it's on and mouthing the words."

And he was right. When "Truly, Madly, Deeply" came on, Dinah was quite capable of singing along with Savage Garden.

The love song fest continued until they reached I-75 and eventually exited into Mackinaw City, stopping at Alexander Henry Park.

Dinah gazed at the lights of the Mackinac Bridge—a five-mile suspension bridge connecting the upper and lower peninsulas of Michigan. So close, the massive structure intimidated her, but it remained an architectural wonder.

"I wanted to stop here because I've never seen the bridge at night and I wanted to share it with you," Arlan said.

"I've never been here. Period. I think this calls for a selfie. Bring your phone." She opened the door, and the chilly wind made her draw her cape around her. At the edge of the parking lot, she said, "What do you think of here?"

Arlan slid his arm across her shoulders and tapped his

phone's camera, flipping to selfie mode. "On three: one, two..."

"Three," the couple said together.

"I'll send it to you," Arlan said.

"I'll see it when I'm allowed to use my phone." Dinah smirked and pulled Arlan in for a slow, intense kiss, full of every emotion she felt for him.

"Very nice, but we need to get going. We're just over halfway there." He walked Dinah to the passenger side of the car and nestled her in the Prius' warmth. Once he entered the driver's side, he plugged in his phone and re-queued his playlist, starting with number eight.

"Whitney Houston? You know I love her, right?" Dinah exclaimed.

Arlan nodded. "I've watched *The Bodyguard* with you, babe." He grasped her hand and brought her knuckles to his lips.

He's put so much thought into this playlist.

More miles passed, and they drove away from Mackinac City.

"I didn't know Elvis did 'Always on My Mind,'" Dinah said.

"Same. I'd always thought it was just a Willie Nelson song."

They sang along with the tunes as the Prius ate up the miles. As they turned into a small motel that had fallen into disrepair, the most perfect tune played.

"Your Song" by Elton John gathered all the thoughts and emotions Dinah felt and wrapped them all up in a beautiful melody.

When he parked and shut off the car, Arlan looked at her. "Oh, babe. Why're you crying?" He pulled her close and cradled her cheeks between his hands, wiping away her tears with the pads of his thumbs.

Dinah took a deep, shuddering breath. "It's— It's such an amazing song for us. Thank you so much for this playlist." She leaned forward and kissed him.

Moments later, Arlan pulled away. "You're welcome. Let me get us checked in. I'll be right back." He leaned across the console and kissed her cheek.

After only a few minutes, they opened the door to the hotel room and stepped into the 1950s. The decor and fixtures exuded the days from long ago—before either of them was born.

"This is...."

"Retro. Very retro." Dinah nodded.

"I was going to go with 'interesting'," Arlan said.

"That works, too."

AFTER ARLAN SET temporary wards in the hotel room, he turned to Dinah. "We need to get up pretty early, and I want you to sleep well," Arlan said as he removed Dinah's cape, thick sweater, black jeans, and camisole, leaving her in lacy undergarments that should have been illegal.

"I have an idea for a sleep aid," she said as she giggled.

"Oh, orgasms are definitely on the menu. The question is: How would you like to come?"

Dinah gasped, then her surprise melted into a shy smile. "How 'bout you decide? I'm not partial to one method or another."

"Got it," he said as he divested himself of clothing.

She stepped into his arms when he reached for her, pressing her warm, silky skin against him. Planting tiny kisses on his chest, she worked her way up to his collarbone and then pulled his head toward her, seeking his lips.

Her kiss started out sweet and innocent but gathered heat and propelled itself into a tsunami of passion.

As the moment intensified, Arlan ran his hands down her sides and to the middle of her lower back, where he pulled her toward him and relished the pressure against his cock, sandwiched between their bodies.

Pulling away from her, he feathered his fingers over the roundness of her breasts, holding them in his palms and running the rough pad of his thumbs over her nipples.

"Oh, Arlan," Dinah said, pressing her thighs together. "You are so good at this. Take me to bed," she said as she stepped toward the mattress, flipping back the comforter and letting it drop to the floor before peeling back the blanket and top sheet, settling with her hair splayed across the pillows like flames licking at the edges of his sanity.

"Dinah, you're the most beautiful woman I've ever known," he said between kisses and playful nips to her thigh.

"Oh," she uttered as Arlan breathed across her mound. "I— I think I need you inside me."

"Shit shit shit. I have to unpack the condoms."

Their eyes met and held, connected for one beat, then two.

Dinah said, "I'm pretty old to be having a child."

"I don't think so, but what I think doesn't matter," Arlan said. He rocked against her, longing to slide into her slick walls.

"I just finished my period—I shouldn't get pregnant, anyway," she said.

Arlan froze. "Are you sure?"

She nodded. "Plus, I've been on birth control for more than a month now." A grin split her face, causing her cheeks to bunch up so tightly he thought they might burst. "Looks like I had a surprise for you, too."

Slipping the head of his member into the entrance to her passage, he paused. "You're sure?"

She nodded. "Oh, yes. Hurry—it feels like I've waited forever for this," she said, breathless.

Nudging his way inside, Arlan paused, getting used to the intensity of the sensation.

Dinah whimpered. "Oh, please—make me come." Her hips rolled and ground, looking for that *just right* position to push her over the edge into oblivion.

"You've got to let me control this, baby. It's so much—too much, maybe." Arlan focused on the texture of the sheets, the soft lighting, and the way Dinah's eyes shone, filled with passion and need.

"Just a little more. Oh, there—there." Timid at first, she slid her hand between them and took charge of her pleasure, rubbing her clit as her hips rocked, intensifying his short thrusts.

And bringing him so close to the brink, he froze. "Dinah. Just a minute. Stop."

She stilled.

Arlan exhaled slowly. "You feel so, so good, baby. Give me a beat to… get myself together so I don't cut this short."

"I don't care. Fuck, I'm so close." She moved her fingers again and a low moan started in her chest as her thighs trembled.

With three strokes, he buried himself in her wet, pulsing sheath as he came deep inside her.

"I'm so sorry," Arlan began.

"For what?" Dinah said and then kissed the tip of his nose.

"That wasn't at all what I had in mind for tonight."

"It was just what we needed, baby. Thank you." She pulled him toward her and brushed her lips over his. "We have forever to make love all night. You said it yourself—tomorrow is an early morning."

"That I did. I suppose we should get some sleep." He kissed her forehead.

"Thank you for whisking me away. I guess I never realized how 'on' I am all the time."

Flopping over onto his back, Arlan said, "You have had so much pressure on you for the past seventeen years. I don't know how you did it. But that's over now. Plus, I'm here to share the load."

Dinah pulled the sheet and blanket over herself and curled onto her side, facing him. "Thank you. I never knew being in love could be like this. And I'm so glad Faith has us as a model of what relationships should be like."

"You're welcome—but I think I should be thanking you."

Dinah's eyes fluttered closed and then flew open. She smiled and her eyes drifted closed again.

She fought sleep.

Then she sat up. "I need to pee and then come back to bed. Do we have any bottles of water?"

"I brought in a cooler," Arlan said. "I'll have a bottle next to the bed for you, and I'll get the alarm set for six thirty—is that enough time if we need to leave by a little after seven?"

Dinah got up and walked across the small room to the tiny bathroom, containing the toilet and bathtub-and-shower combo. "That's fine." She peered at the tub. "It's not like we're going to get busy in *this* shower." She shut the door.

He opened the bag Faith had packed for her and pulled out her hair supplies, make-up remover, and toothbrush, setting them on the sink.

Then he moved to the small cooler on the floor and unzipped it, retrieving a bottle of water for Dinah and one for himself. Arlan opened both bottles and downed one of them. He capped the other and set it on Dinah's side of the bed.

Arlan went about pulling out his charging cord and finding a working outlet so he could plug in his phone overnight. He set the alarm and triple-checked that it was set for AM and not PM.

Dinah emerged. "Oh, you didn't have to get out my things. Thank you," she said after washing her hands.

"Bring your brush over here," Arlan said.

"I can—"

"I know you can brush your own hair, but I want to do it."

"But—"

"But nothing." Arlan held out his hand.

Dinah smiled and sighed dramatically. "I suppose. If you must." She plopped onto the edge of the bed next to him.

Arlan clambered to the center of the mattress and

kneeled, giving himself room to complete each stroke of the brush from her scalp to the ends.

"I'll let you do this all night—but we...er, *I* need to get some sleep, or you might regret it in the morning." She twisted and reached out for the brush. In a few quick swipes, she set the brush down and made quick work of plaiting her hair into two neat rows, twisting a small scrunchie around each end.

"Why do you braid your hair at night?" Arlan asked.

"It makes it easier to brush in the morning. As you know, I can be a wild sleeper," Dinah responded.

"I don't know about that. Faith said you sleep a lot better now."

"I used to have a hard time with sleep and night terrors."

Arlan nodded. "You've not had one of those when I've stayed over."

Dinah looked away. "And you don't want me to." She sighed. "Anyway, let's get to sleep. I need my beauty rest." She scrambled onto the bed, pausing to kiss him and nudge him toward his own side of the bed. Once she settled, she took the bottle of water and drank half of it.

Arlan nestled in and pulled up the covers, opening Dinah's side, inviting her to fall asleep in his arms.

She didn't have to be asked twice.

After turning off the lamp, he said, "I love you."

She whispered, "I love you, too." On her next exhale, her body melted into his, and he could tell she was sound asleep.

.   .   .

THE WARNING SIREN of his alarm startled Arlan awake.

Dinah flailed around and sat straight up in bed, the blankets pooling at her waist, revealing her tempting breasts.

No time for that this morning.

He shut off the offensive noise and grasped Dinah's hands. "Hey, you're safe. It's okay."

Her terrified expression softened into recognition.

"There you are. Good morning." He kissed Dinah before getting out of bed. "Do you need the bathroom first?" he asked.

She shook her head. "I'll get dressed and go right before we leave."

"Okay."

Within thirty minutes, their bags were packed, and the car loaded.

"The front desk said there's nowhere to get coffee this early, so we'll have to deal with these bottles of iced coffee I picked up, just in case."

Dinah smiled; tiredness etched across her face. "You think of everything." She took her bottle and opened it, taking a sip. "Ah. That'll do until we can get something better."

After taking his own sip, Arlan said, "I heartily agree."

Not long after, they pulled into Huron Shores Roadside Park.

"What are we doing here?" Dinah asked.

"I wanted to watch the sunrise with you, and I thought over Lake Huron would be beautiful."

Dinah squealed. "This is something else I've never

done!" She launched herself over the console and wrapped her arms around his neck, squeezing.

After a few moments, Arlan said, "You stay put for a minute or two—I've got a big comforter in the back. It's going to be chilly."

Dinah settled back in her seat. "Worth it, to watch the sun rise with you. Thank you."

When he opened the door, he glanced back at her before getting out.

She wiped away tears trekking down her cheeks.

"Hey, this is a good thing, right?" he asked.

She nodded. "These are happy tears."

"As long as they're happy tears, that's okay."

After pulling the comforter out of the back end, he opened Dinah's door and wrapped the blanket around her as she got out. He kept her bundled up as they walked across the grass toward steps leading down to the beach. *If all else fails, we can sit on the bottom step.*

The water lapped against the shore as the push-pull of the waves lulled Arlan into a sense of peace.

Swooping toward them, a seagull let out a mighty *screeeech*, causing both Arlan and Dinah to jump.

"Beach chicken," Dinah grumbled.

"Flying rat," Arlan murmured.

They looked at each other and started laughing.

"Before we settle on the ground, let's do a selfie—before the sun rises," Arlan said.

"You're so s-s-sweet," Dinah said, shivering.

"I'll be quick and then I can get inside the covers with you and help keep you warm." He held out the phone, after switching to the front-facing camera, and said, "Ready?"

Dinah nodded.

"One. Two. Three." He snapped the picture and Dinah whipped the comforter open, pulling him toward her.

The duo waddled down the beach a bit and settled against a washed-up log that looked like it had seen many sunrises in that exact position.

Pinks and reds appeared along the horizon and bit by bit the sun made its appearance over Lake Huron.

Dinah, transfixed by the beauty, was speechless.

Once the sun was fully visible over the lake, Arlan said, "So, was it worth it?"

Dinah nodded. "Oh, yes. And I'll do this with you anytime." She turned and kissed him.

"Okay. My brain is saying it's time for real coffee. What about yours?" Arlan asked.

Dinah nodded. She pushed away the blanket and stood, her cape flapping in the breeze. She walked toward the rocky shore, peering at the stones. Then she gathered the outer garment and squatted, picking up something. She rose and looked at him, holding out her treasure. "Arlan! I found one! A Petoskey stone!"

And there she was—the vision of Dinah from his dream—drifting across the sandy beach wrapped in a forest green cloak, her eyes glimmering in the haze of the rising sun emerging from the water.

bewitched by bourbon

A Teachers' Lounge Paranormal
Romance, book two

about the book

**Get ready to be bewitched by this intoxicating blend
of paranormal romance and small-town charm.**

Maddie Kelly thought she had it all figured out. A talented
chemistry teacher with a knack for distilling bourbon, she
was finally ready to spread her wings. But life in the small
town of Zephyr was about to get a lot more intoxicating.

When Jonathan Mann arrived to open a new distillery,
Maddie's carefully balanced world began to spin.
Suddenly, her magical abilities were acting up, her
bourbon experiments were yielding unexpected results,
and her heart was racing for reasons that had nothing to
do with her past struggles.

As Maddie and Jon's relationship heated up, so did the
danger surrounding them. Jon's deranged ex-wife and his

reservations about sharing the not-so-nice parts of himself threatened to shatter their newfound happiness. With her family's legacy of witchcraft and her own inner demons to contend with, Maddie had to decide if she was ready to risk it all for love.

In this enchanting tale of magic, bourbon, and second chances, Maddie discovers that sometimes the most potent spells are the ones we cast on our own hearts. Will she have the courage to embrace her true power, both as a witch and as a woman? Or will the ghosts of the past prove too strong to overcome?

prologue

"All I'm saying is that Zephyr would be a great place to start a bourbon distillery. There's a natural spring on the property I'm looking at, and we can get all the resources we need up here. What do you think?"

Maddie's ears perked up when she heard the words *bourbon distillery.*

"Jonathan, you *know* I adore you, but I'm not sure Zephyr is the right place for you to move to. It's…" Mara Slade—art teacher—looked around and made eye contact with Maddie before turning back to her friend and continuing, "…a little difficult to get 'in' here, if you know what I mean."

Madeline Kelly, chemistry teacher, refilled her coffee

during her prep period and tried to avoid looking at the man who had the potential to make her dreams come true: working at a start-up distillery.

Months passed and Maddie had forgotten about the overheard conversation when Mara sidled up to her as she walked down the hallway a week before exams started.

"So, do you remember the very attractive man with a voice like *whoa* who was talking with me in the lounge back before the winter holiday break?" Mara asked.

"As matter of fact, I do. He was talking about starting a bourbon distillery up here, wasn't he?"

Mara nodded and then looped her arm through Maddie's, walking shoulder-to-shoulder down the hallway. "Well, he's doing it and he's looking for some local people to work for him. It'd be part time to start, obviously."

"I— I don't know, Mara. I'm getting my own place, finally, and that's a pretty big step for the summer. I definitely have time, but the new job might be too much for me."

"I'll text you the URL for the 'Careers' page of the website. You might have noticed that they've got a new cabin built on the Bălan property and they've remodeled the barn a bit. If the microbiologist role is for you, you can apply. I think you'd really like Jon Mann—he's honest, fair, and an all-around great guy."

"Thanks, Mara. I'll take a look, but I'm not promising anything."

"Oh, definitely. If this isn't the time for you, it isn't the time for you. I remember hearing you mention traveling to Kentucky to do some summer apprenticing at bourbon distilleries, so I thought this might be one of your once-in-a-lifetime opportunities."

It is a definite dream job for me, and it doesn't require me to move away. Couldn't hurt to take a look at the posting and apply, right?

Did you enjoy this excerpt? Get your copy of *Bewitched by Bourbon*, the second book in the Teachers' Lounge Paranormal Romance series, today! Visit our store: https://payhip.com/PurplePenWords

acknowledgments

I think I must start by first thanking my family:

- Mr. VampBard—you have given me time and space to write the books of my heart.
- The Spawn—you've been the best cheerleaders!
- Dad & Sis—your words of encouragement have meant the world to me.
- and Mom—who always knew I could do it.

And this book DEFINITELY wouldn't have been possible without my writing mentor, Maddie James. Along with Lucinda Race, we're the Scribe Sisters. Your support and responses to "how does this sound?" were exactly what I needed. Thank you.

Finally, my co-working team. Monday through Friday, I open up a Zoom room at 10 a.m. Eastern and keep it open into the afternoon and evening some days. Mary, Mia, Michelle, and Rudy—y'all have kept me accountable to myself and without each of you, this book would never have been finished and edited.

about deelylah

and Puck, who thinks he's a co-author

Deelylah Mullin is the pen name for full-time <u>freelance romance editor</u>, Wendee Mullikin. Since 2010, Wendee has been living her best life with her very own romance hero, Mr. VampBard. Between them, they have six grown Spawn (adult children) plus their significant others, two grandchildren, two grand puppies, and a grand kitty.

When she's not writing or editing kissing books, Wendee and Mr. VampBard enjoy traveling the state of Michigan, where they reside. Waterfalls, lighthouses, and historical markers, oh my! Big water, a.k.a. the Great Lakes are Wendee's happy place, and there's nothing better than listening to the gently lapping waves in Lake Huron, the rolling surf of Lake Michigan, or the crashing waves on Lake Superior (she doesn't get to Erie & Ontario, much).

Keep up with what's going on in the Teachers' Lounge series and other titles written by Deelylah Mullin by signing up for her newsletter: https://www.purplepenllc.com/dm-nl

bookbub.com/authors/deelylah-mullin

facebook.com/deelylah

instagram.com/vampbard

threads.net/@vampbard

tiktok.com/@vampbard

also by
deelylah mullin

The Teachers' Lounge series

An Apple for the Teacher

Bewitched by Bourbon

Visit our online bookstore: https://payhip.com/PurplePenWords